Night Train

Als ik 's morgens door de verlaten natuur fiets, merk ik dat ook de taal me verlaten heeft. Ik heb geen woorden tot mijn beschikking, ik heb ze niet nodig. Later, als ik alleen op mijn kamer zit, zijn de woorden terug, maar ik gebruik ze niet om te praten, want ik ben alleen. Ik gebruik ze pas als ik ze ga schrijven en lezen. Soms worden ze vertaald en kom ik in een vreemde dierentuin. Een ezel wordt een zebra, een muis wordt een vleermuis, een pad wordt een paddestoel, een vink wordt een slavink, een olieman een olifant, een olifant een nijlpaard. Ik ben in een wereld gekomen die ik herken, maar die niet de mijne is. Ik ben rijk geworden, maar mijn buurman merkt het niet.

A. L. Snijders

Night Train

translated from the Dutch
with an introduction
by Lydia Davis

NEW DIRECTIONS
PAPERBOOK

Night Train is published by arrangement with AFdH Publishers, the Netherlands. Special
thanks are due to Paul Abels and Martien Frijns for their help: many of the stories collected
here first appeared in their bilingual 2016 volume, Grasses and Trees.

First published as New Directions Paperbook 1513 in 2021
Manufactured in the United States of America
Design by Erik Rieselbach

Library of Congress Cataloging-in-Publication Data
Names: Snijders, A. L., author. | Davis, Lydia, 1947– translator, writer of introduction.
Title: Night train : very short stories / A.L. Snijders ; translated from the Dutch with
an introduction by Lydia Davis.
Description: New York : New Directions Publishing Corporation, 2021.
Identifiers: LCCN 2021022085 | ISBN 9780811228565 (paperback) |
ISBN 9780811228572 (ebook)
Subjects: LCGFT: Short stories.
Classification: LCC PT5881.29.N53 N54 2021 | DDC 839.313/64—dc23
LC record available at https://lccn.loc.gov/2021022085

10 9 8 7 6 5 4 3 2 1

New Directions Books are published for James Laughlin
by New Directions Publishing Corporation
80 Eighth Avenue, New York 10011

Contents

The Very Short Stories of A. L. Snijders

I. DISCOVERING SNIJDERS

For most of my life, I have worked as a translator from the French, but I have also translated from other languages, including some I hardly knew—a linguistic adventure. In May 2011, I visited Amsterdam for the first time and came away with the idea that I would like to translate something from Dutch literature into English. The idea was born of the notion of reciprocity: a Dutch publisher was bringing out a book of my stories, translated into Dutch. Could I not, in return, translate at least one small piece of fiction from Dutch into English?

In fact, the idea may have suggested itself even before that trip. A couple of years earlier, I was teaching a writing class that happened to have a very international student enrollment. Two of the students were fluent in Dutch. I had the previous year been published in an issue of the Dutch magazine *Raster* devoted to the very short story. I was trying to decipher some of the other stories in the issue: one of them, by Hedda Martens, was a retelling of the story of Rumpelstiltskin which I thought I should be able to understand, but even after some hours of struggle I was not having much success. I never did go on. Yet it seemed possible—after all, a number of the words were recognizably close to English and German, which I already knew.

After I came back from Amsterdam, I wrote to several people I had met, asking them if they would recommend a writer of very short stories I might like to translate. I was looking for stories of just a page or two, since each page would take a concentrated effort. Two correspondents wanted to draw up a comprehensive list for me, but since they had children and school vacations were just beginning, they said they would write again in the fall. A third, however, emailed me promptly, and that was Vincent, who had hosted my husband and me while we were there in Amsterdam, walking us back and forth along the canal on Herengracht between the house in which my publisher had its headquarters and the hotel where we were staying.

Vincent recommended A. L. Snijders, who had been writing very short stories for many years with, at that time, more than 1,500 to his credit and still counting. He had in fact invented his own term for what he wrote—zkv's, short for *zeer korte verhalen*, or "very short stories." He had recently been awarded a major prize. Vincent sent a story by Snijders with his email. It was about Snijders's mother falling out of a window when she was a year old and surviving with no ill effects, her fall having been broken by an awning. I understood only a little of the story, but enough to know that I liked Snijders's straightforward approach to storytelling, his modesty and his thoughtfulness. I was also grateful for his short and fairly simple sentences, his avoidance of subordinate constructions, and his choice, predominantly, of concrete rather than abstract nouns.

I checked with one of my other correspondents for her opinion of this writer, and she said, "Snijders's work is full of regional/cultural/political/literary references, it is sometimes more like what we call a column (a short piece in a newspaper with an opinion), so it must be selected very carefully. I like it very much."

An added incentive for finding some very short Dutch stories to translate was the desire to respond to submission requests from literary magazines not always with a story of my own but, instead, with a translation—preferably from a language I did not know well since it was new territory and therefore a greater challenge. A translation from French, for me, always has its own set of challenges, but they are altogether different from those of a language I'm still learning at a beginner's level.

I read that first story by Snijders ("Years") over and over again. I chose to read it first without a dictionary, since I found I was more deeply inside it that way, figuring out what the words meant from the context, and enjoyed it more, since it was like doing a word puzzle without looking up the answers. In that story, I was able to understand at least one sentence without help: "We kennen elkaar niet, twee vreemden." Using the context and cognates—probably a neat enough formula for attempting to understand a language without prior knowledge of it—I deciphered it to mean: "We do not know each other, two strangers." *We* is the same word in English; *kennen* is a cognate of the Northern English dialect word "ken," meaning "know," as in a song I have heard from my childhood on: "D'ye ken John Peel with his coat so gay?" about a Cumbrian hunting-farmer of the early nineteenth century. (The song tended to romanticize hunting; in the 1970s, antihunting activists vandalized Peel's grave.) I'm not sure how I figured out *elkaar*, unless I was guessing from the rest of the sentence. *Twee* is a cognate of "two," and *vreemden* a cognate of the German *fremd*, "strange, foreign."

I continued to work on it, still without a dictionary, "getting" a little more of it each time I read through it. Simply reading a sentence carefully a second time yielded more understanding—I'm not sure exactly what happens in the brain between the first and the second readings.

Within a few days, I had made a rough version of that first story. Vincent helpfully said he had plenty of time to look at my translation, because, where he was, it was *komkommertijd*—the meaning of which he challenged me to figure out: "good luck on that one," he said. I knew that *tijd* meant "time" (as our cognate "tide" also did, back in the sixteenth century). I imagined, of course, that *kom* and *kommer* had something to do with "come": perhaps, in the Netherlands, it was "come-comer time"; anyone might come by and take up some of his time, his time was available for whatever might come along. No, in fact it meant "cucumber time," late in the summer when the cucumbers are ripening and people are less busy, or away.

II. SNIJDERS

A. L. Snijders was born Peter Müller in 1937 in Amsterdam, one of six children. He tells us a little about his parents and siblings in "The Heart of the Story," how they were a conventional bourgeois Catholic family and how his older sister decided abruptly to turn her back on that life, the city, and the Netherlands itself. The city and its neighborhoods appear in that story and in many others, including "Luck," about his youthful music lessons; "Years," about his mother's fall from the window as a baby; "Rozenstraat," about an art installation and a canary; "Ox," about a language discussion in a food store that also, indirectly, involves national identity and immigration. After attending art school, with ambitions to be an artist, and after holding a few other jobs, Snijders found a more permanent position teaching in a police academy, where he remained for many years. He married, had a family of his own that also included five children, and, in 1971, moved to the Achterhoek, a quiet, wooded region in the east of the Netherlands where many of his stories about animals and about his home life are set.

In describing his school years, Snijders admits that he was never a good student and that, in particular, he could never write long sentences. Although he was bright, had a sharp memory, and worked for a time as an assistant to one of his professors, his style was criticized as being "too lapidary." (He went and looked up the word: short, pithy, as though hewn from stone.) He went on, however, to make a virtue of necessity, as he explains in the story "Shoe," and developed this style into one suited to writing very short stories.

In the 1980s, Snijders began writing newspaper columns in this peculiarly Dutch genre—short, opinionated, combining observation and imagination, sometimes fable-like, sometimes political and sometimes moral. It is a form used by other notable writers in the Netherlands, each with his or her own twist, but also, in their own varieties, by other European cultures. (One highly interesting practitioner, for example, is the Swiss Peter Bichsel.) In 2001, Snijders began sending out by email his so-called zkv's, which had evolved from the columns. In 2006, AFdH Uitgevers published his first collection of zkv's, bringing him quickly to a wider public attention. More collections followed—to date there have been eleven collections and a staggering total of over 3,000 stories.

In November 2010, Snijders was awarded the Constantijn Huygens Prize, one of the three most important literary awards in Holland, in recognition of his work as a whole and especially his zkv's. Soon thereafter, he began reading regularly for the radio every Sunday morning.

Besides reading them at public events and on radio and television, and collecting them in books every few years, Snijders also continued, right up to the day before his death this year, to send his stories out to the email list called the *graslijst*. Earlier in his life, he used to write a story every day, sometimes even two, in about half an hour, with few or no corrections. Then he reduced his output a little, to four stories per week, for different outlets, one of them the very local newspaper in his own hometown which is distributed free door-to-door (to about 500 readers). He apparently placed as much importance on publication in the local paper as in one of his other outlets, *De Standaard*, one of Flanders's most important newspapers (distribution about 500,000).

More recently, feeling the stress of so much productivity at his age (eighty-three), he cut back to writing one new zkv every other week, to be broadcast on the radio to his approximately 70,000 regular listeners. (The intervening week, an older story was read.) He would write it on Saturday and read it aloud at 8:45 the next morning. He read aloud on the radio weekly for about ten years. Reading the story took five minutes, he said, and (somehow he knew this) most of his listeners would set their alarm clocks for 8:45, listen to the story, and then go back to sleep. In all those years of reading on the radio, he missed his appointed time slot only twice—once when he fell ill and a second time after his wife died unexpectedly.

When asked about revising the stories, Snijders said that he sometimes made changes in a story before reading it aloud on the radio, but preferred not to. In earlier years he never changed anything, but rather wrote very slowly (*schreef zeer langzaam*), in order to make no mistakes. As time went on, he wrote more quickly (*schrijf sneller*), made more mistakes, and corrected them.

I was sure that he did not publish all of the stories but must select the best or have the selection made by his publisher, both for his books and for his email list. But this turned out not to be true, either. Paul Abels told me Snijders chose not to select, but to include all, and so the publishers followed his lead: every story has been published. Abels told me that Snijders might publish a story the way he used to bake bread. He would bake a loaf of bread every day. He would say, You have to eat every day. So you bake a loaf of bread every day, and if you baked it, you eat it.

Another assumption needed correcting. I was sure, from the beginning of my acquaintance with Snijders's stories, that they were all true, taken with no changes from his life, only shaped in small ways. Then I encountered a story that could not have been altogether true: in "Accountant," as he is searching for his glass eye, which has fallen out (Snijders did not have a glass eye), he meets and talks to a man, an accountant, who reminds him that he, the accountant, in fact exists only in a dream. This upended my assumption; now I had to wonder about the other stories. And it is true that in "At the Intratuin Garden Center," for instance, he comes upon a naked couple in the pond and aquarium section, standing clasped together not far from a table manned by a cluster of guerilla fighters under the command of an Indian woman— this might also have given me doubts, though until now it did not. I had faith: maybe the scene was a piece of impromptu theater; what did I know about Dutch garden centers?

Yet I might have been enlightened by some quite direct statements Snijders makes in some of the stories. In "Baalbek," which at first seems to be about his desire to travel, he goes on to declare that he has "another wish: for reality without reality—stories that are indistinguishable from the truth." In "Shoe," he is even more explicit:

> At first I am always inclined to write what I have heard, blunt reality is my source. But sometimes there are obstacles ... The remarkable thing is that readers notice I've left reality behind, I imagine readers notice ...
>
> (That's nonsense, of course, readers can't notice, I'm the only one who knows. Yet I sometimes do have the idea that readers notice.)

I was one of those readers who continued, or preferred, to believe that most of what I read in his stories was true, and his publisher seemed to confirm this, or rather—maybe an important distinction—stated that most were "based in reality" (though names were fictitious). Again, however, when I asked him, Snijders himself clarified: no, in only about two hundred of the stories is there no fiction at all.

III. TRANSLATING SNIJDERS

I soon found myself on Snijders's email list, receiving the stories at just the right intervals so that they took me by surprise and induced me to start reading. First thing in the morning, I would look at my emails and might find a new story. I would sometimes start a translating a story even before my first cup of coffee. I would begin by trying to read the story. I would read the first line. More than once, it contained the word *bosrand*, "edge of the woods"— something Snijders sees from his kitchen window and a place I like to be, in my imagination. Or it contained something about the author's problematic chickens, or his dogs. One began with a woman (*vrouw*) in the distance ("distance" is *verte*, which, confusing me for a moment, is identical to the French for "green," but whose root is *ver*, sharing a past with the English "far"). Still half dreaming, I would be transported to the Dutch countryside, among the chickens and buzzards, foxes, shepherds and swans, and the occasional cyclist or hiker coming along the *pad* (cognate of "path") in front of the author's house, or *huis*—actually pronounced more or less like the English and the German *Haus*.

> Some words are, to my ears, comical, such as *sla*, meaning "salad"— it sounds cool and casual. I am reminded of "slaw" in "coleslaw" though I'm not sure they have a common source. When I look it up, I learn that *sla* is a shortening of the French *salade*. And that our "coleslaw" is in fact an importation of the Dutch *koolsla*, "cabbage salad."

If I ran into too many words I didn't understand, or if I wasn't interested in the subject (rare), I didn't go on. But if I could read and understand most of it—if I could begin with *Ik zit aan tafel onder de lamp met mijn wollen muts op mijn hoofd* (here, I had trouble with *muts*, which looked nothing like "cap," and *hoofd*, which did not suggest to me that, like its German cognate *Haupt*, it means "head") and figure out most of what followed, and if I liked it (usually the case), then I might feel that translation urge taking hold of me.

> *vrijgezel: vrij-gezel*: I'm amused to see that the word for bachelor includes the word *vrij* (cognate, G. *frei*), meaning "free." *Gezel* = mate, partner. *Gezelschap*, cognate of German *Gesellschaft*, means "society." I think of the Bach-Gesellschaft—the nineteenth-century Bach Society that published Bach's complete works, the editing of some volumes faulty, some very good.

In my peaceful *tabula rasa* state of mind, I would copy the text from the email and paste it into a new file, then type in the title and the author. I would start on it immediately, typing the title in English above the Dutch title, and then the author's name again under the English title, and then the first sentence: "When the roosters crow in the distance I want to go off on a journey," or "Above the path in the woods behind my house where I walk every day I see a buzzard flying among the great beeches," or "It began with . . ."—and refer back to the Dutch: *Het begon met bomen, het eindigt met stenen.* At that moment, translation, which I've found, over the decades, to be so infinitely complicated, would seem very simple. It would seem to be exactly what it is so often misunderstood to be, by those who have no experience of it: all you need to do is read the text and then write it in English.

> *vijf*—if I'm forgetful or careless, I read it as "wife"—I am reading too fast and the word is taking a quicker, reflexive pathway to my English translation; I should be reading a little more slowly and thinking, before I jump to the translation. After all, I have known for some time that "wife" is *vrouw*, like the German *Frau* and, since *v* is pronounced like *f*, pronounced almost exactly the same—also, I actually know the word *vijf*, which means "five" and is pronounced almost the same: "fife."
>
> Another wrong guess: *fles*, which in fact means "bottle." I was at first thinking of "flesh," related to the German *Fleisch*, "meat," but the cognate in this case was "flask." We also have "flagon," which seems farther away but is actually derived from the same source. Why are so many *fl-* words in English associated with liquid (or . . . flowing fluid)?

Because I was tempted by these email offerings, which kept coming, I would almost always start on a new Snijders story before I had finished the others. In this way, I accumulated many partial translations, spread out on my computer desktop, in different stages of completion. I kept them visible so they wouldn't get lost and forgotten in the large folder (containing still more drafts of translations) labeled "Snijders in progress." Eventually, one by one, I finished respectable versions, sent them to be checked by a Dutch reader, usually Snijders's publisher, Paul Abels, and incorporated his suggestions.

In one Snijders story, the *sleepboot* is not a "sleep boat" or "sleep boot" but a "tugboat"; the Dutch *slepen* is a cognate of the Yiddish *shlep*, which also means to drag, carry, or haul (but with the added implication, of course, that this hauling may be unnecessary or at least tiresome and reluctantly done). So we could say "schlep boat." And *sleeppad* has nothing to do with a pad for sleeping on, but is rather a path for schlepping—a towpath.

Dutch appealed to me, on the page, anyway. It is not too hard to learn if you know some German. Also, English has the great advantage—for learning other languages, and especially for one's own writing—of its enormous doubled Latinate / Anglo-Saxon vocabulary (two words for everything: subterranean / underground; terrestrial / earthly; submarine / undersea; celestial / heavenly). The Latinate vocabulary gives an English speaker some access to the vocabulary of the Romance languages, while the Anglo-Saxon vocabulary gives some access to the vocabulary of the Germanic languages. For learning Dutch, having some French also helps now and then in construing an imported word, such as the hedgehoggy *pruik* (derived from the French *perruque*, wig) or the onomatopoeic *put* (derived from the French *puit*, meaning "well," and perhaps imitating the sound of a drop of water). There are also similarities between some Dutch vocabulary and some already familiar words in Scots and the dialects of Northern England.

Sometimes Dutch-English cognates have letters reversed: *borst* = breast; *pers* = press (the media); *vers* = fresh (*v* pronounced as *f*). And maybe also, though I'm guessing now, *vors* = frost.

No, when I check, I see I am wrong about the last one: it turns out that although the Dutch *vors* did indeed reverse letters as it evolved, it derives from *frosk*, and is an archaic word for "frog."

I think now that although German always seemed closer and more familiar to me, it may in fact be harder for me to learn than Dutch, maybe harder for anyone to learn. Dutch, for example, has only two words for "the"—*de* and *het*—whereas German has three in the nominative singular case alone (*die*, *der*, and *das*), never mind the genitive, dative, and accusative singular and the plural forms of all those.

I liked being transported to another place and another culture. Also, I liked the sound of the Dutch words in my head—as I imagined them. (In actuality, I was surely pronouncing them quite wrong. During one of our walks back and forth along the Herengracht, I tried over and over again to pronounce just the little word *van* correctly, under Vincent's coaching, but could not get it right. To pronounce the name Van Gogh correctly would take still more practice.)

> *ondoorbrengbaar scherm*: here is quite a mouthful, but I think I can figure it out, since I recognize all the parts of it. The first thing is to break the long word into its shorter component parts: *on-doorbreng-baar*. This produces "un-through-bring-able." Since the word is paired with (modifies) "shield" (*scherm*), I can guess that it means "impenetrable." My association with *scherm* is the German *Schirm* which is most familiar in *Regenschirm*, screen or protection against the rain. Our "umbrella" has a very different provenance and climatic association: it derives from the Mediterranean (Italian) *ombrello*, "little shade"—the protection, there, is from the sun, not the rain. "Parasol" is really the same idea: *para + sol*: "protection against the sun." The French for "umbrella," now that I'm thinking about this, is *parapluie*, returning to the idea of protection against the rain, and, with *pluie*, we're also back to the sound of the drops of water.

One of the surprises I had, as I tried to figure out the word without help, was that some Dutch words translate directly, not into our Germanic equivalents (such as *kurkdroog* into "cork-dry") but, more deviously, into the component parts of our Latinate equivalents. For instance, I encountered *onderwerp*, did not understand it, tried separating it into its parts, *onder + werp*, both of which I understood—"under" and "throw"—and then, since it was a noun, moved it around to make some peculiar thing called a "throw-under." This made no sense. When at last I looked it up, I found that it meant "subject"—which is indeed "thrown-under": it is derived from the Latin *subjectus*, *sub+jectus*, which means just that, "thrown under." In our familiarity with "subject" and the way we habitually use it, we forget its concrete origins.

> An idiom—*kurkdroog*: *kurk-droog*, literally, "cork-dry." But we would say "dry as a bone." Why do we prefer bone to represent dryness while they prefer cork? Cork trees are not native to England or the U.S., but it isn't that—they're not native to the Netherlands either. (Using cork stoppers in bottles, however, goes far back in all three cultures.)

When I turned to a dictionary for help, the one I used, at first, was very small (a little over 2″ × 4″), yellow, faux-leather-covered, a Hugo pocket version for travelers which I'm guessing my mother bought for a trip she took with my brother to Amsterdam in the mid-1960s. The cover is torn a little at top and bottom, though the book is sturdy and won't fall apart. Some pages are stained and a few are missing, evidently ripped out. Since these print-covered pages wouldn't be useful for writing a hasty note, I can only imagine they were removed to be used as bookmarks, but that seems a little odd. If there is another explanation, I'll probably never know what it is.

> Some words contain cognates to older forms of our words. There is the Dutch *dorst*, for instance. It is a cognate of our "durst," past tense of "dare": in chronological order, I suppose we would have said, and written: he durst not say anything; he dared not say anything; he didn't dare say anything. The Dutch for that is: *hij dorst niets te zeggen* ("he durst say nothing"; literally, "he durst nothing to say").

I continued to use this dictionary if I was reading a Dutch book on a bus or a train, even though something electronic would have been quicker. Maybe I liked the little interval of time between putting down the Dutch text and leafing through the dictionary—which then sometimes didn't have the word, after all, either because it is such a limited travel dictionary or because of those missing pages. In that interval, I might look out the window for a moment or at the visible parts of the other passengers. When I was at the computer, though, I used about three different online dictionaries, each of which had its own strengths and weaknesses. If all of these failed me, I did a general internet search for the word or phrase and found it in one of a variety of contexts (though sometimes, of course, the only reference was to the very same piece of writing by Snijders that I was translating), and thereby gained some feeling for Dutch life and culture, reviewing the hours and stock of a chain store in Rotterdam or the specifications of different brands of tile stoves or the almost incomprehensible scraps of teenage conversations.

Here is a new word, not seen before: *oeroud*. First reaction: no idea! (That is often the first reaction.) Then I return to it with more patience. The beginning of it—*oer*—reminds me of some of our ae-words, such as aerate, which also look strange to me; and because the word contains *roud*, I can't help thinking of "round." But I seem to remember that *oer* means "over," although some of these words, along with their meanings, do tend to drift in and out of my memory, and now I recognize *oud*. The context is a description of some stony terrain by the Black Sea, and this word is an adjective qualifying the trees there—*oeroud* trees. The second part of the word, *oud*, means "old"—close to the Northern English dialect *owd*, as in *Owd Bob*, the classic English novel about sheepherders and sheepdogs set in Cumbria. *Oud* is also part of the Dutch word *ouders*, meaning parents, or "elders." "Over-old"—I can guess that it means "very ancient," but I will wait and see if any more understanding comes, or I will simply capitulate and look it up.

When I do look it up, I see that it does mean "ancient," but that I was wrong about *oer*, which does not mean "over" (the Dutch for "over" is in fact *over*) but is related to the German (by now, in fact, our own word, too) Ur, meaning primordial or primeval. The trees are primevally old.

A fair number of the stories contain only material that needs no footnoting, for instance, the people and animal life out in the country where Snijders lived—the neighboring farmer, the foxes, the chickens, a shepherd, a bird-watcher. But quite a few of the stories, as one of my correspondents had warned, are full of proper names. At first I thought this would be a problem in translating his work, creating the Scylla and Charybdis between which I would not be able to steer safely: either the story, in translation, would be scattered with unfamiliar and unexplained references, or it would be cluttered by notes that would add to the page a cast of the academic that might hurt the vitality of the stories.

But then I saw the references in a more positive light. I would not want to leave them unexplained, after all, since they were so rich in meaning for both Snijders and his Dutch readers—I would include notes, but put them at the back of the book where they would not interrupt the reading. And as I did my research for the notes, I would learn something about Dutch history, geography, and literature, as would eventually, in turn, the reader of the translations. Snijders often refers to, and quotes, other Dutch writers—in fact, in his modesty, sometimes the greater part of a story will be a quotation from another writer. And these are, most often, not obscure figures, but important earlier writers, such as Nescio or Gerard Kornelis van het Reve—two of his inspirations—or contemporaries of Snijders's such as Gerrit Krol, Joubert Pignon, or Nicolaas Matsier. For serious readers in our Anglophone culture not to know at least the names of these writers seemed a lack that might be made good. And why should we not also know something about the Netherlands' popular TV show hosts (Jan Wolkers, for two years, gardening program), right-wing politicians (Geert Wilders), Amsterdam cafes (Vertigo, named after the Hitchcock film), Dutch dialects (Low Saxon), or Middle Dutch epics (*Reynaert the Fox*)?

zeehond: divided into its two parts, it is *zee* + *hond*, or "sea + dog" (cognate: "hound"). I'm guessing that it is "seal." (Confirmed, when I look it up.) Which reminds me of the story a Scottish friend of mine told me, about how, on the coast of Scotland, a certain dog would come running down to the beach every afternoon at the same time and plunge into the surf. Offshore, waiting for him, was always the same group of seals, who gathered there at the same hour. The dog and the seals (the *hond* and the *zeehonden*) would play together in the water for a while, maybe half an hour, and then the dog would return to the beach and the seals would swim away.

But besides Dutch writers, in keeping with Snijders's wide reading and curiosity, we come upon those of other countries and cultures. One of the most moving stories, "Oh My Bride," is titled after, and quotes, a poem by the English poet Stevie Smith. Isaac Babel's gangster Benya Krik makes a brief appearance in another story (Babel is another important writer for Snijders). In "Poem," Snijders relates how he thanked a lenient young traffic cop by reciting to him a short poem by Kawabata. A favorite phrase from *Moby-Dick* appears in "Pussyfoot," and a story told by the American poet Charles Simic is related in "Suckling Pig."

In Snijders opens "Carbide" with a paragraph from "The World of Apples," a story by John Cheever. Since I had the habit of not reading ahead to the end of a story before beginning to translate it, I did not see that Snijders was not the author of the paragraph, and so I earnestly did my best to take it from Dutch into English correctly and idiomatically. Only when I reached the second paragraph did I see what I was doing. But this immediately interested me, as well, since it was an opportunity to examine, from the inside, what happens to a text when it is translated—in this case, what happened twice, really. My version in English was quite all right, accurate and natural. But the differences between my version and the original Cheever in fact confirmed what we know, but should be even more alert to, about translation: that it very often—though not always, in the best translations—levels, generalizes, bleaches out, robs the original of some of its color, character, luster, and eccentricity. The translator tends to opt for the standard or generic rather than the regional or peculiar, and, quite rightly, is wary of injecting his or her own personally idio-syncratic language into the translated text, thus tending to flatten it out.

A first example from the Cheever paragraph is not too egre-gious: "As he approached the river" became, in Dutch, "Toen hij bijna bij de rivier was" and then, in my English, which was closer to the Dutch, "When he was nearly at the river." The original Cheever continues with a particularly nice verb: ". . . a little Fiat drew off the main road." The Dutch, "reed er een kleine Fiat van de grote weg af," chooses the verb "drove," more generic than "drew," and, again, my English translation, correct but bland, fol-lows the Dutch: "a small Fiat drove off the highway." Or perhaps not so correct, since a "main road" is not the same as a "highway." One other example, in this passage: Cheever's "shotgun" be-comes, in Dutch, "geweer," more standard, again, than Cheever's English, and I translated it as "rifle"—correct but not as powerful or individual as "shotgun."

*

Snijders, in his stories, is personal but with the same keen, objec-tive interest in his own everyday activities as in the world beyond himself. He gives us fragments and facets of his life—one Dutch literary critic and commentator, Florian Duijsens, has called his form "autobiographical fable" and points out that cumulatively, as we hear about Snijders's boyhood, youth, early teaching career, adventures on the road, and friends, the stories form one very long newspaper column, or, to change the metaphor, constitute so many pixels of one whole image. Snijders depicts the world close to his home: his family, his neighbors, chance encounters with strangers—a wood seller, a hitchhiker, or a passerby stopping in at his house—but the subject he returns to always is the animal world and its variety of creatures, with whom he lived shoulder to shoulder (and sometimes, abruptly and uncomfortably, eye to eye) and whom he portrays with respect for their different and unknowable ways of seeing and thinking, and with awe at their inherent mystery.

In "Forty Centimeters," for instance, a story about his chickens that begins quite simply but ends with several questions, he quotes from an essay by Gerrit Krol that discusses whether pecking behavior is learned or innate: "Innate, says one half of science, because it pecks while still in the egg. Even in the egg, says the other half, you can learn something." Krol continues: "Scientifically speaking . . . both views are correct," and Snijders concludes: "Because I have no talent for science, I am always very happy with these last four words: *both views are correct.*"

> False friend: the *haan* in the poultry yard, in a story by Snijders, is not a hen, but a rooster or cock. The hens, along with some roosters and some chicks, regularly entered Snijders's stories, because they were a part of his everyday life, and that is, at least in part, what he writes about.

But his subject matter also ranges farther afield, to the geographically more distant world, other places in Holland and in foreign countries, places he still frequented or remembered from his past or associated with friends or correspondents. And then, in this widening circle, there are the larger realms of his many interests—music, philosophy, sailing, politics, food, motorcycles, language itself, and especially other writers. In all his depictions, there is wit, wonder, a gentle humanity inflected by his strong and compassionate political convictions, coupled sometimes with a hint of irony. There is color; characters appear and disappear, there for only a moment but fully alive.

Formally, these stories have in common their brevity, but beyond that, their structure and pacing are various, some of them no more than an almost static snapshot, some a neatly rounded narrative, and some a meander. In these, as in "Forty Centimeters," in fact, a story will begin in one place, with one apparent subject, and then wend its way to quite a different conclusion—reflecting the patterns of our own erratic trains of thought. Another of this kind is "Geese," which begins with a pair of geese that are either there or not, in the field by his house, and ends with a difficult teacher of his, memory, and mortality. Yet another, one of my favorites, partly because it develops so naturally, is "The Baker's Wife," whose title announces what Snijders meant to be the subject of the story until something else came along to push that one out of the way. In this case, Snijders circles back for a moment to the baker's wife at the end. But we are not given her story. And since I haven't read all of his stories, I don't know if he ever did write it.

> *Vele schouders maken het werk lichter*: not hard to decipher via cognates, including one from German: literally, "many [cognate is G. *viele*] shoulders make the work lighter." Compare the English version of the same expression: "Many hands make light work." Hands versus shoulders—is this because the Dutch used to carry fish, vegetables, seaweed, and perhaps other things in baskets slung from yokes which lay across their shoulders? The German version of the expression is more rhythmical, and rhymes, and has a slightly different perspective: *Viele Haende machen bald ein Ende*: "Many hands make soon an end."

Now Snijders has died unexpectedly, in early June of this year. His publishers, Paul Abels and Martien Frijns, when announcing the news, reported that as Snijders sat at his desk on a Saturday, in the midst of writing another *zkv* to be read the following day, his heart simply stopped. A few days later, the publishers sent out the unfinished story to his *graslijst*. I'm sure I'm not the only one who was grateful to have the story but will let a little time pass before reading the very last words Snijders wrote.

Translating Snijders has been an adventure, a years-long excursion. I have had the privilege of living with his country and culture, his great variety of subject matter, his quiet sense of humor, his nuances of thinking, his flexibility of form, his linguistic curiosity, his wide embrace of culture, history, literature, and his surprising conclusions. And his questions—when a story ends with a riddle, or a doubt, as many of his do, the subject of the story becomes, in part, Snijders's own questioning, or more broadly, our own shared habitual uncertainty, perhaps even the shared uncertainty of our human existence. I find this a natural, and thus comfortable enough, place to land, or to poise, just as I find such apparent honesty in writing as Snijders's, and, especially, honesty about uncertainty, always admirable and, rightly or wrongly, trustworthy. I am sorry that I have, so far, managed to convey into English only these ninety-one stories, out of thousands, but I look forward to reading many more, witnessing over and over the combination of observation, long study, long experience, and fertile imagination that have yielded each of their particular, individual moments of humor, insight, or philosophical bewilderment. And I regret that Snijders's life was so abruptly cut short—as it feels, despite his advanced age—when surely he had many more stories to write for us. His death is a painful loss to the literary and cultural life of the Netherlands, but also far beyond.

LYDIA DAVIS
JUNE 2021

Night Train

STORY (3)

The train from Zutphen to Winterswijk is quiet, few passengers. Yet the new man comes and sits down directly opposite me, I have to pull my legs in. I am on my way to the Mondrian Museum, where a drawing hangs that has never been shown before, it has always lain folded up in a drawer. It is not by chance that the man has chosen this seat, he wants to talk, he has a story to tell. It is clear that he is not interested in the unknown drawing by Mondrian, he looks defeated, he wants to tell the story, I nod, let it come. He says he wants to smoke a cigarette. Don't, I say.

He tells me he has a great love, his neighbor's wife. He has been fond of her for years, and she of him, but they have never expressed it, they have never touched each other. She is married, has a pleasant, indolent husband and a little daughter, it seems to him a good marriage. Their spiritual, adulterous love is on a higher plane, it approaches the mystical. I look at his tormented face and ask him what happened. She moved away, he says, her husband was transferred. He saw her once more, in the train. There they held each other for the first time, there they kissed and wept. Never again did they see or speak to each other. I know it, I say, it's a story by Anton Chekhov, you're telling me a story by someone else. I know, he says, I know that story by Chekhov, but I did not read it until my own adventure was in the past. It was a shock that I had lived in a story by someone else. Do you think Chekhov invented it? With writers, you never know, I say.

GRANDSON

I don't know if my Canadian grandson Jack is a Buddhist, but he certainly looks like Buddha. Also, he loves peace and philosophy. In most children's TV programs there is a lot of activity and noise, he doesn't like that. He is a lover of the tomfoolery that goes on in Jan Wolkers's gardening program. Of him, he says: "That man knows about animals." Nota bene: He is two years old.

GRASSES AND TREES

I am seventy-three years old, people expect me to say wise things about old age. I don't do that, men of eighty must do that. The Japanese draftsman Hokusai wrote:

> Starting in my sixth year of life, I was obsessed by drawing the forms of things. Starting in my fiftieth, I produced a great deal, but nothing that I made before my seventieth year was really worth the trouble. Only in my seventy-third did I at last begin to see something of the essence of birds, animals, insects, fish, and the vital nature of grasses and trees. This is why it is only in my eightieth that I will have registered some progress, that when I am ninety I will have penetrated farther into the deeper meaning of things, that in my hundredth year I will be truly extraordinary, and that in my hundred and tenth every dot and every line will possess life itself.

I have a neighbor, a boy seventeen years old, I see the passion with which he holds his girl. I think: What a lot you will know when you are a hundred and ten.

JAARTALLEN

In 1912 valt mijn moeder in de Van Eeghenstraat van driehoog uit het raam. Haar moeder komt de kamer binnen en ziet dat het eenjarige meisje op de vensterbank is geklommen en tegen de hor leunt. De hor valt naar buiten en het kind erachteraan.

Hoewel haar moeder verlamd is van schrik, rent ze naar beneden. Haar dochter is ongedeerd, ze heeft geen schrammetje, zoals men in zulke gevallen zegt. De hor heeft de straat eerder bereikt dan het kind, is teruggesprongen en heeft haar val gebroken.

Op 14 januari 2008 parkeer ik mijn auto om half twee 's middags in de Van Eeghenstraat en fiets naar het Blauwe Theehuis in het Vondelpark, waar ik een afspraak heb met een fotograaf. De fotograaf is ook op de fiets, we zetten ze tegelijk vast aan het hek. We kennen elkaar niet, twee vreemden. Pas bij het theehuis ziet hij dat ik ik ben, en zie ik dat hij hij is.

Het theehuis is in 1936 gebouwd, een jaar voor mijn geboorte. Het is guur en regenachtig weer, ik heb mijn wollen muts op. Hij maakt de foto's. Hoofd iets hoger, nee, ietsje terug, nu omdraaien, kijkt u maar in de richting van de Van Eeghenstraat. Ik kijk en denk welk raam. Ik zeg tegen de fotograaf: daar is mijn moeder in 1912 uit het raam gevallen.

Als hij klaar is, fiets ik naar Vertigo (Duizeling), waar ik koffie drink. Ik denk aan mijn dode moeder, wat zou er van haar geworden zijn.

YEARS

In 1912, my mother falls from a window three stories up in Van Eeghenstraat. Her mother comes into the room and sees that the one-year-old girl has climbed up onto the windowsill and is leaning against the screen. The screen falls down and the child after it.

Although her mother is paralyzed with fear, she runs downstairs. Her daughter is unharmed, she hasn't a scratch, as people say in such cases. The screen reached the street before the child, rebounded, and broke her fall.

On January 14, 2008, I park my car at half past two in the afternoon in Van Eeghenstraat and go by bicycle to the Blue Tea House in Vondelpark, where I have an appointment with a photographer. The photographer has also come by bicycle, we fasten them to the fence at the same time. We don't know each other, two strangers. Only once inside the tearoom does he see that I am I, and I that he is he.

The tearoom was built in 1936, one year before my birth. The weather is bleak and rainy, I have my woolen cap on. He takes the photos. Head a little higher, no, back just a little, now turn, can you look more toward Van Eeghenstraat. I look and wonder which window it was. I tell the photographer: my mother fell out of a window there in 1912.

When he is finished, I ride my bike to Vertigo (Duizeling), where I have a coffee. I think about my dead mother, and wonder what has become of her.

OLD PRICK

Nico and Klaas are friends. Nico has interesting cats (Abyssinian, Siamese). Klaas has a sailboat. They hang out at the gate of . . . let's say Oosterpark. They complain and talk, they're friends, especially after sunset. Klaas is eager to take a little trip in his boat (seven meters, polyester), he wants to go to the West Indies, he wants Nico to go with him. Nico thinks about his mortgage, a broken crown, his wife and his seven interesting cats. Klaas says that just once in one's life a person should do something he can look back on with pride. Nico hesitates, he thinks that seven meters isn't very large and that polyester would not hold up against a dozing whale, a boat should be made of steel. Klaas disappears without saying goodbye, Nico hears nothing more from him. After half a year a picture postcard arrives from Barbados. "I'm here, you old prick, and it's just the way I imagined it." The familiar drama of dream and action, what you should do, how you should live.

I could have invented this, but I did not, I read it in the paper, in February of this year, 2008, sitting on the floor, somewhat desperate. I was cleaning up, papers from the past, at that time violent, exuding ardor—now tame, resigned, flames subsided. Newspapers, too, ardent dancers in the current affairs of one day, were now endearing. (There is something fraudulent in this process, for example you read that a world war is imminent. You know it never came closer, you feel a sort of sympathy for the people who were afraid at the time, you feel you are a part of Progress, you forget that progress doesn't exist.)

The story about Nico and Klaas is in the issue of *Het Parool* dated Friday, June 3, 1988, very yellowed, almost brown in my hands. Nico Merx is a columnist. His column that day begins:

> The postman brought a card sent from Barbados. The picture side showed a beach with palm trees. On the other side was a single sentence. "I'm here, you old prick, and it's just the way I imagined it."

34

BECAUSE HIS WIFE

The rooster is as old as a crocodile. You can measure the age of the earth by the covering on his legs, by the look in his eyes, by the wattles under his beak, by his shrinking comb. From a youngster in a burlap bag he has become a priest, *sacerdos, sacerdos*. When he crows, you can hear that death is a catastrophe. Yet this is only part of the myth. *Because his wife* ... His wife is a chicken, just as old as he. Brown at one time, but now completely white (I repeat, and I'm not lying, that this chicken has gone from brown to white in her color-changing chicken-life). Long ago she stopped laying eggs. Nature, say the experts, such is nature, it's natural. But now the white chicken has started laying again. The day before yesterday one egg, and yesterday another.

FOX

Although in the '60s I studied with Hellinga, the greatest expert ever in *Reynaert the Fox*, I had never yet seen a fox in the wild. (Because I studied with Hellinga, the greatest expert ever in *Reynaert the Fox*, I had never yet seen a fox in the wild.)

Now within a short time I have seen two foxes. The first was a scrawny creature in our garden. I was standing in front of the window, he walked calmly past two meters away. I cried out in agitation and yelled in a high-pitched voice: "A fox, a fox." Actually, I had already known he must be there—a couple of weeks earlier three chickens had been killed and one rooster mutilated—but *to see* is different from *to know*. Some time after that, one morning, I looked out my bedroom window and saw a handsome specimen with a large tail walking tranquilly back and forth at the edge of the woods, nose to the ground, searching for mice. When I went toward him a bit later with the dogs (one loose, one on a leash), he saw me. He did not run away, he went and sat down and looked at us, his ears pricked. At the distance that his nature dictated to him, he turned around and walked slowly to the edge of the cornfield. There he went and sat behind the first row, clearly visible. Only then did I understand why he has become such a prominent figure in world literature.

SEAGULLS

I'm raking piles and piles of leaves in the garden. Eight chickens are walking around me, pecking up worms and larvae. This makes no impression. What makes an impression is when I stand at the stern of a ship and watch the seagulls flying along. That's how it should be.

OX

The Croissanterie Jennifer is in Raadhuisstraat. There I buy two pistolet rolls with *ossenworst*—ox sausage. The shopkeeper takes the rolls out of their little basket using a paper napkin. Even when he's spreading butter on them, he does not touch the bread with his hands. He cuts the ox sausage in thick slices, which he lays in place with a fork. This is done carefully, he takes his time. I read on the blackboard that here it's *ossoworst*. He asks if I'll be eating it here. I say I use the car for that. The man was not born in the Netherlands, there is an air of refinement about him. I'm guessing that he's from Egypt. I hesitate as to whether I should say anything, there are so many possibilities—condescension, pedantry, socialism, pro-Wilders sentiment, humility, pride, compassion. I say: "It's called *ossenworst*, it's *worst* (sausage) from an *os* (ox), do you think it's wrong of me to say that?" He says: "No, I think it's nice when the Dutch concern themselves with me." The sentence is like a sharp knife. He says: "What is an ox?" I say: "A castrated bull." A veil hangs over his eyes. I make graphic motions with my hands: balls off, no longer male. He thanks me. I pay up: 5 euros 40.

PASSION

He told his daughters about passion, but they did not want to know anything about it. They left him at daybreak and walked for ten hours without resting to the seashore. There they stayed for three months, they helped with the beach chairs and tents, and they made music to earn money. But when war threatened they walked back home, where their father was still preaching about passion. Now, because they had grown a little older, they wanted to know about it in detail, they wanted to know all the details concerning passion. They sat down by him and addressed him using the word "father." He explained to them how they should live, what they should do. They should aim their lens at an arbitrary goal, they should hold tight and not let go, they should pay no attention to the head-shaking and the words "Well, she has a nerve!" This was how they should live, this way things would turn out well. The daughters were furious that a father should dismiss the matter so easily, as if he were teaching a course in an educational center. They advised him to stop using words and left the house for the second time. At the beach they saw the dredgers and excavators that were strengthening the coast, but they sat down with their feet in the sand because it gave them such a delightful feeling.

SHOE

Often a zkv is just a very short story. Sometimes it is a real zkv, in which case the letters zkv no longer mean anything. Then it has become a shoe that pinches a little, the content is (slightly) larger than the form. The difference must not become too great, no binding, no mutilation, no beautiful little Eastern foot.

In primary school, in high school, at university, everywhere, I was among the worst students, with the lowest grades. In silence I engaged in polemics with the head group, I did not submit to this injustice of fate. What annoyed me above all was that I could not write long sentences. I developed a fear of the anacoluthon. I had a sharp memory: I was a teaching assistant to Hellinga and had to write little reports. His comment was: "Too lapidary." I believe I looked up that word, short, pithy, texts hewn from stone, lapis / stone.

Much later I made a virtue of necessity, I began to write very short stories and noticed that brevity could be 1) technical in nature—few conjunctions, little explanation, trust in the reader's autonomous cerebration—and 2) substantive.

(*Inopiam ingenio pensant* = to make a virtue of necessity.)

"Passion" is substantively a zkv. I sit in company with others at the table and hear a man claim that one must live with passion, with a goal, with perseverance, unwavering—I hear his wife mumble, "That awful word, it can still make our daughters furious." At first I am always inclined to write what I have heard, blunt reality is my source. But sometimes there are obstacles, I leave the table, I go sit on the beach—the passion, the father, the daughters must do it, I follow. The remarkable thing is that readers notice I've left reality behind, I imagine readers notice. Those are the real zkv's.

(That's nonsense, of course, readers can't notice, I'm the only one who knows. Yet I sometimes do have the idea that readers notice.)

JEALOUSY

Jealousy is a vulgar feeling, but I suffer from it. Paul comes by with his Moto Guzzi California, it is early in March, the sun is shining, spring is blinking her eyes. I go downstairs when I hear the enticing sound of the motorcycle, I see it leaning to the left on its slender kickstand, I am jealous, I want to ride through the springtime on a motorcycle like that, too, the way I rode to Durgerdam fifty years ago on my BMW. The world lay open before me, but I rode to Durgerdam, deep ditches, buttercups. Paul even comes inside for a moment, he takes off his helmet, his leather jacket, too, but he leaves on the leather trousers and the leather boots. We drink coffee and talk about motorcycle riding. He invites me, he lures me, he tries to tempt me, he wants me to ride the Moto Guzzi just a short distance, in order to have that feeling one more time. We don't know it, but we're talking about life, we're talking about time, we're talking, without knowing it, about the victory of time. I refuse, I decide that I'm not twenty years old anymore, I decide I won't die on the battlefield like that. As he rides away, I go stand in a place where I can still see him for a long time on that splendid Italian bike, he rides under the lindens, he waves.

Late in the afternoon, he sends me a message. Twelve kilometers before Enschede he hears a bang, he is going 120 kilometers an hour, 4,000 rpm, he maintains control, steers onto the median, waits for help, sitting on the guardrail. There's a hole in the engine the size of a silver dollar. In the garage, all the mechanics come and take a look when the Moto Guzzi is put up on the lift. They have never before experienced this. One connecting rod is stuck in the right cylinder, a pulverized connecting rod, the crankshaft reduced to smithereens. With a magnet, they fish pieces of cast iron out of the crankcase, like shark fins from jet-black soup. One mechanic says: "The rear wheel could've got jammed, too. How fast were you going, again?"

Everyone thinks about fate, chance, narrow escapes, none of us move from where we are, none of us know the final answer. I think: This could also have happened in Durgerdam—in 1957.

HURT TO THE BONE

My oldest friend is named Bob van Aken. I first met him in 1947 or '48 in Roompotstraat, we were ten or eleven years old at the time. I remember clearly what I thought: this is the nicest kid in the world. Sometimes I saw him every day, at other times I never saw him. When a couple of days ago I was sitting in Wildschut at the corner of Van Baerlestraat and looking toward my grandma's window and toward the bookstore Het Martyrium, I also looked obliquely into Ruysdaelstraat and thought about Bob van Aken's girlfriend. I believe she has been his girlfriend for a very long time, but I've never seen her or spoken to her. This morning, he called me up and told me that he always parks his bicycle under the awning of Het Martyrium, next to a girl's bike that has been standing there unused for four years. He did not tell me why, but a man can think, he is free, there is nothing to stop him, so I thought: he puts his bike next to the other one out of *solidarity*. That notion is too narrowly used—Gaza, Greenland, whales and chimpanzees—but it can also flow like oil through your head (although here I must immediately make a marginal comment: when that feeling of solidarity becomes oily, there is the danger that you will begin to love all of humanity). He had called me up for no reason, so we talked yet again about the sentence that we both rate as one of the best:

> Bastard, a country preacher who made pitifully little progress in life, published his book in 1598. It was regularly ridiculed. Bastard died, hurt to the bone, in a debtors' prison in Dorchester.

(This is Bob's number one sentence, I put it in second place. My gold medal goes to Flaubert's observation that nothing can exist without bitterness, that there should always be a whistle of scorn when we triumph and that our enthusiasm always goes hand in hand with despair.)

AT THE INTRATUIN GARDEN CENTER

naked man by koi carp, woman on shoulder.
milk spilled on milk factory driveway

This is written (without capital letters) on the scrap of paper that proves I bought something at Intratuin (two bags of potting soil, cashier name: Mirella). I have written it down so that when I'm back at home I will remember that in the pond and aquarium section I saw a live naked man standing there carrying a live naked woman. He stood with his front against the front of the woman, who hung upside down with her thighs on his shoulders and her head between his knees. I was not just surprised, I was alarmed. I looked around, there weren't many customers, it was ten o'clock Tuesday morning. Farther on, four men wearing the caps and jackets of guerilla fighters sat behind a large table watching, completely intent. On the table stood apparatuses that were unfamiliar to me, next to the table stood a woman from India who was apparently the commander.

I left the section quickly and did not ask for an explanation at the cash register. Next to Intratuin there is a cement factory and a milk factory. The driveway to the latter was covered in milk. That was just too much. A leaky milk truck, I said to myself.

PLEASURE

I looked out through the kitchen window over the snowy fields. I saw a hare sitting in the distance. I had human thoughts about the hard ground and the frozen grass. Then suddenly the hare began to run. There was no danger, no dog at the edge of the woods, no buzzard in the sky—everything was gray and silent. The hare ran in a straight line, faster and faster, he was enjoying himself, he did it out of sheer pleasure, I was sure about that.

RESENTMENT

When I go out to the chickens in the morning, I don't see a single one. They have walked through the thick privet hedge and are sitting at the edge of my neighbor's meadow. In the sun! Which is hanging in its winter guise just above the horizon. The chickens are enjoying the little bit of warmth. Although I take pleasure in the scene (I have walked around and I'm watching them from the pasture), I suddenly understand where my resentment comes from: I find them ungrateful. They run free, their surroundings are varied, I give them an abundance of food, I don't mistreat them, but they offer nothing in return. That is ungrateful. I could also deceive them with lifelong imprisonment, a light-clock and artificial warmth, I could subject them to the economics of Jan Kalff, and then they would thank me with a daily egg. But now I treat them well, I suffer for it. The source of my resentment is my thoroughly humanistic outlook on nature.

SUMMER

On Labor Day I was in fact working. I had my overalls on, it was 82 degrees Fahrenheit, I was outdoors. I was making a floating roof out of galvanized corrugated iron, which I had bought for ten euros a sheet from a scrapyard. While I was paying, the junkman had tried to persuade me to vote for Peter R. de Vries in the upcoming elections and I had also half promised this to him for reasons of expediency, but while I was building the floating roof, I decided to break the promise after all, because on further reflection I felt that casting my vote for this man would be particularly uncivilized. As I worked, I was witness to a deafening incident. At the edge of the woods, on the ground in the meadow, a buzzard was busy tearing apart his prey. In the trees perched a hundred or so crows, cawing loudly. The buzzard was also being attacked, in low-flying swoops. He was unmoved. Sometimes he struck out with a wing when they came too close, but casually, as though it had all been foretold already. The main sign of summer is the mewing (really, the *meowing*) of the floating buzzards. Ever since I have lived here (starting in 1971) this has signified summer.

BAALBEK

For more than fifty years I have cherished one wish: to travel. This wish is part of another wish: for reality without reality—stories that are indistinguishable from the truth. I often set out on a trip, I put everything in order and drive off early in the morning. I always want to go to Baalbek, to listen to the roosters of Lebanon. I have a neighbor a couple of hundred meters up the road. I have never spoken to him, but he waves when he sees me. He has a rooster which I sometimes hear crowing. As I approach his house, I am overcome with anxiety and I go back. I don't think I'll ever see Baalbek.

NOTE

A little piece of paper fell out of the cupboard. A timeless and undated note. I read:

> It's odd that almost everything you may communicate about some-one is more interesting than his face. Take a complete enumeration of someone's wardrobe. That seems to me, especially in the case of a contemporary, highly interesting. Or an inventory of someone's possessions: "Besides his clothes, he owned an IBM typewriter, two gold ten-guilder coins, a 1966 Austin Balanza, thirty-five acres of woodland in Westfalen, a house on the boulevard in Zandvoort, stocks worth eighty thousand guilders, a savings bank deposit book showing twelve thousand guilders. Sometimes, as he calculated his assets, he also included the five hundred guilders that he once, at a Rotary meeting, lent to the mayor and the return of which he did not dare ask for." This is when a person appears to you distinctly.

It was written in my own handwriting, but I couldn't imagine that I had made it up myself. I turned it over, on the other side was written "note by Karel van het Reve."

I thought about the Turkish boys, two of them—students, I was their teacher. They wanted to see my house. I said no. They asked why not. I said that you shouldn't go looking for reality, that as much as possible you should leave room for imagination. They said that I could come to Turkey anytime, I would be welcomed by their parents, I could eat and sleep in their home as long as I wanted. I felt overwhelmed by their natural hospitality, but I did not want to let go of my little theory. I said I would never go to Tur-key, because I wanted to fantasize about Turkey. I said my feet and eyes and nose were marvellous pieces of equipment but stood in the shadow of my imagination. I said they should not take it per-sonally, I had just recently been invited by a friend to visit Odessa with him and walk through the streets of Benya Krik, but I had declined that too, with the same argument, I preferred to dream about Benya Krik.

The two Turkish police trainees came after all, on a summer evening, in uniform. The dogs ran at them, but the two young men showed their Dutch passports and called out: good people. The dogs quieted down.

Why I think about this after reading the note by Karel van het Reve, I don't know.

MINOR CHARACTERS

I'm visiting a scholar in linguistics and literature whom I've known for fifty years. The path we once shared split like a snake's tongue, he became a professor and I did not. But now we're at the end, he an emeritus, I a pensioner, our differences have blurred and we are talking frankly. I say that I have the greatest admiration for people who can write a thick novel, and I add quietly that I too will try it sometime (because I want to admire myself). He does not laugh, but strongly discourages me, he says I shouldn't do it because I understand nothing about psychology, "not even the psychology of the minor characters." That is handsomely formulated, I promise him I will not do it. But that night in bed I think that perhaps I actually could write an unpsychological novel for all the people who also understand nothing about psychology.

BALDUR

On page 193 of the second edition of the cult book by Carel (CV, CH) I read:

> The grandfather of Baldur von Schirach, Friedrich Karl von Schirach, fought in the American Civil War as major in the Northern army and lost a leg in the Battle of Bull Run. When President Lincoln was murdered, he stood guard by the coffin on a leg made of cork. That leg must have been an orthopedic wonder, for after the Civil War, the major danced at all the great balls of Philadelphia.

I experienced World War II and therefore know who Baldur von Schirach is, but if you were born after 1945 and you happen not to have an encyclopedia in the house and you are also not connected to the internet, then you won't have a clue.

LUCK

When I was young I played the recorder, I took lessons from Kees Otten, who lived in a large house on Koninginneweg. These opulent houses were formerly lived in by wealthy families, but after the war, mothers and daughters from Russia and Poland lived there, as well as poor musicians, poets with office jobs, students. For Kees Otten you had to go up ten flights of stairs, he gave the lessons under the rafters, you looked out over Vondelpark. Sometimes I had lessons at the same time as Simon Castaris, who played alto recorder and was in love with a girl who worked in a magazine shop on Beethovenstraat. Simon had met her at the fair and treated her to a ride on the Caterpillar, where he kissed her. After that he thought she was his girlfriend, but she was not that kind of girl. And so he often went to gaze at her in Beethovenstraat, toward closing time, when darkness was falling and he could see her clearly in the light of the shop. She often saw him standing there and was touched by him because of his defenselessness. With this tenderness, love returned, thwarted, however, by Vondelpark. Simon lived on the prosperous side, and his love on the Overtoom side, in a common little street, another world. She preferred him to take up the accordion, and that happened too, I no longer saw him at the lessons with Kees Otten. Years later I met him one more time, he was through with that girl and with music. The accordion and the alto recorder lay at home waiting for new musicians. I yearn for the stories the recorder can tell over a hundred years—who, in that time, blew their poetic breath through that wooden body? For musical instruments can live longer than people, with a little luck, and I suspect they are also endowed with better memories.

ULK

I thought my chickens were killed and dragged away by a fox, but now I doubt it. An ulk seems more likely (*ulk* is Achterhoeks for polecat). I have a friend in this neighborhood, he's from Amsterdam, like me. We still have big-city fears. (Freud is unknown in the country, people think it's a brand of milking machine.) He has chickens too, in a large, sloping run with an artificial pond, everything he does is a little more chic than what I do. For instance, he's a poet, whereas I'm a writer—it's a subtle difference. One summer night he hears screeching. He jumps out of bed, grabs his powerful lantern and a stout stick. He runs to the chicken coop, naked. A large number of chickens are dying and dead. The murderer is still there, he's sitting against the wire netting in the light from the lamp, he can't get away. His assailant comes closer, stick raised, the animal prepares himself, his eyes see death, his teeth are bared. But the man fears for his penis, original castration anxiety. He lets the animal escape. Which he is right to do.

BUZZARDS

I'm afraid of dogs, except when I'm their master. We have a guest here, a strong, black street dog from Amsterdam, who walks around unleashed there without getting hit by a tram. His master is on vacation in Patagonia, the dog is staying here and does not do what I tell him to. When I open the door in the morning, he runs to the woods without looking back, while I yell "stay here." He's not deaf, but he understands that I'm not his master. After a couple of hours he returns, usually wet and muddy, because he loves water. There's something else—it's too quiet for him here, he's a street dog, he's used to the tumult of the world. When a cyclist passes our house (the path belongs to the house, the notary has a legal document about this) I see rage appear in the dog's eyes, I can barely hold on to him. I take a precautionary measure, I put him on a leash. When I'm behind the house, I hear an unpleasant uproar on the path, the dog has torn himself loose and has torn a hiker's pants to shreds. The man says the pants cost 150 euros, I pay, though I myself have never worn such expensive pants. When the vacation in Patagonia is over, I feel good, I sit in my iron chair and listen to the buzzards mewing high up in the air. That is the sound of summer, everything else is very still.

MICE

A mouse inside a shoe is not a primal fear, not a trauma, but I do pay attention, all the same. It's because of the open roofs. I have a house with three tile roofs. They used to be haylofts, they were not timbered, the wind had to be allowed to blow through freely, against the heat and damp. Time and purposes change, I timbered one roof, gas was installed, the electricity went underground, drainage pipes were laid, but the mice stayed. The house is in the fields, there are mice everywhere. A rare owl has been spotted in our country, it comes from Germany, where there is a shortage of food (for owls), there are too few mice there. We live in the midst of great movement, oil, energy, mice, people, water. You can see it on television, you can't understand it, or half of it at most, but you can see it.

I have two lodgers, cats belonging to my daughter, who is driving around Sicily in a rented car. Every morning there are dead mice lying in the guest room, the cats are young and diligent. Soon I will have to fight the battle alone again, the vacation will be over and they will be back in Amsterdam, where there are almost no mice. Yesterday in a forgotten cupboard I found two pairs of shoes. I recognized them, old, but still usable. First I hold them by the tips, and I shake them—to be absolutely sure, I even poke them with a little piece of wood. Then I put them on; once my feet are inside them, I feel ten years younger, but that doesn't help, I'm still thinking about oil, energy, mice, people, and water.

ROZENSTRAAT

On Good Friday, the canary waits, unnoticed, in Rozenstraat. He doesn't know what he is waiting for, that is his tragedy, and also mine. At first, I don't notice him, I'm looking at the installation of which he is a part. Installation technique. Rozenstraat runs parallel to Rozengracht. I am in Rozenstraat for the first time in my life—before Good Friday 2008 I had no idea of the existence of Rozenstraat, a long, narrow street in the Jordaan district. At number 59 is the SMBA (Stedelijk Museum Bureau Amsterdam—Municipal Museum, Amsterdam Office), a gallery. ART. My eyes take up position, I am in the presence of ART. The artist is Lucas Lenglet, I know him, that's why I've been invited. He lives in Berlin, where he exhibits his installations. I also receive invitations from Paris and Sweden, he's an international artist. The installation in Rozenstraat consists of a wall of solid gauze, sprayed yellow. On the wall hang gauze cages, boxes of solid gauze, sprayed yellow, one right up against another, the land of Mondrian, De Stijl, the Afsluitdijk. The canary sits deep in one of these cages. I am early, time poisons my life, I am always on time (always on time), I am never late, time holds me in his fist. There is no one standing by the installation, I am alone with the canary, which at first I don't notice, which makes the tragedy worse. I have ten thoughts. Number 8: no one sees the canary. The space fills up in an hour. Number 8 turns out to be incorrect, everyone is looking at the canary. The exhibit is called *a canary in a coal mine*. A lectern is brought in, a man in a hat gives an introduction. He is German, he puts my ten thoughts into words. The first: mankind is the first victor, but also the first victim. You can tell that from the canary.

WOOL CAP

Flip is coming for dinner, I hear his car driving past the house. I'm sitting at the table under the lamp wearing my knitted wool cap, I'm supporting my head with my hands, he can see me. It is a moment of grace, I try to put myself in Flip's soul. What will he do when he sees me sitting like that. Ach, I can already tell, he will not react, he doesn't care how I sit, and besides, although I don't know it he is bringing with him a Japanese poem.

During dinner, Flip writes something on a napkin in English. *It is autumn time / I go nowhere / No one comes here.* This is probably his answer to my wool cap. I ask "Japan?," he nods and scoops another spoonful of small potatoes onto his plate. I ask him who wrote the poem, and when. He says: "I will have to give you the answer to that later, but I can tell you that the little verse can also be read metaphorically." I am dismayed, and say: "Oh God, no, I always simply read what it says."

At eleven o'clock Flip has had enough, he wants to go home. There's a sentence he often repeats: "Well, I've got to go take care of the horses." The advantage of this ritual formula is that it is free of emotion. You don't have to be ashamed or feel impolite. When occasionally he forgets the time and it becomes too much for me, I ask: "Shouldn't you go take care of the horses?" Then he is startled awake, says "Oh, yes," and presses my hand in taking his leave.

When he is gone, I ask myself why a Japanese poem should be in English. I translate: *Het is herfst / ik ga nergens naartoe / niemand komt mij bezoeken.*

The next morning, I receive a message. Subject: Dates for Snijders. The poem was composed by Shohaku, who lived from 1442 to 1527, at the time when here in our country a poem was written about how all the birds had begun their nests. Flip has also done a translation: *Het is herfsttij / ik ga nergens heen / niemand komt langs.*

I find *herfsttij* too pompous, but otherwise his translation is better than mine.

That doesn't matter much to me, I can do masonry better than he can. I carry a ladder out of the barn and climb up to a crack in the wall of my house, where last summer I now and then saw a bat come out. I can take the whole stone out, the hole is empty. I feel justified in mortaring the thing closed, which I then immediately do. Afterward I compose a poem at the kitchen table: *The bat has gone / the man takes a ladder / he mortars up the hole.*

SIX WORDS

In the crematorium, a daughter is talking about her father, who lies in the coffin. I don't know her, I knew him in the last twenty-five years of his life, during the half century before that he was for me an anonymous history book. That happens more and more often, you meet people with an unknown past, perhaps they were fascists or anthroposophists, perhaps they were in prison or in a seminary, you don't know, you have to be careful with your little jokes, you don't know which of their nerves is raw, you don't know who their wives were or where their children remained.

The daughter speaks to her father, sometimes she says "papa," sometimes her voice sings. It is a beautiful, sunny summer morning, the life has come to an end, the age is good, the grief is bearable. I sit by the large window and look at the garden, where a compact Japanese tree stands. I know little about the organization of our country. Who is the owner of the crematorium? A private person who profits handsomely from the fire? A consortium with a mailbox on the Cayman Islands? Or simply the government? That is what I would prefer, I think everything should belong to the government, especially the trains and the mail.

The daughter tells us that as an eighteen-year-old boy her father went off over the water in a little boat to paint and then forgot everything. I think, "How splendid life is." She tells us that for two and a half years he had worked on the moors as punishment, he did not want to be a soldier. I think, "How much men are capable of." She says: "A real father you were not." I think: "What a splendid sentence."

It sometimes happens that language is so seductive that its surface beauty lays a hermetic screen over its content. Thus is the content preserved, a later explanation never penetrates. And so it is with these six words, which have a perfect tone, and a mysteriousness that can come to full bloom only through a farewell.

I hear no bitterness in these six words, they glide gently from a young man who sits painting in a little boat, to a soldier who does not want to fight, to a father who looks on from a distance.

CARBIDE

As he approached the river a little Fiat drew off the main road and parked among some trees. A man, his wife, and three carefully dressed daughters got out of the car and Bascomb stopped to watch them when he saw that the man carried a shotgun. What was he going to do? Commit murder? Suicide? Was Bascomb about to see some human sacrifice? He sat down, concealed by the deep grass, and watched. The mother and the three girls were very excited. The father seemed to be enjoying complete sovereignty. They spoke a dialect and Bascomb understood almost nothing they said. The man took the shotgun from its case and put a single shell in the chamber. Then he arranged his wife and three daughters in a line and put their hands over their ears. They were squealing. When this was all arranged he stood with his back to them, aimed his gun at the sky, and fired. The three children applauded and exclaimed over the loudness of the noise and the bravery of their dear father. The father returned the gun to its case, they all got back into the Fiat and drove, Bascomb supposed, back to their apartment in Rome.

In the night before the last day of the year, I was reading out loud "The World of Apples," a story by John Cheever about the very famous poet Asa Bascomb, who was plagued by lewd, obscene thoughts. At the moment that I read "aimed his gun at the sky, and fired" (half past one), there was a sound of a big explosion outside. I was very frightened. It was the first carbide shot from Eppie Tolzicht, whose house is on the horizon. For the next sixteen hours, he continued to occupy himself with his carbide. I'm very fond of chance, and so when I thought about it again I was not surprised that the first bang occurred after the word "fired."

SATURDAY EVENING

On Saturday, January 7, at seven o'clock, I stand in front of the glass door of the main entrance to the Nutsgebouw on Riviervismarkt in The Hague. To my inexpressible joy, it is indeed seven o'clock. The glass door is locked, in the distance I see a symmetrical scene—in the middle, I see a woman singing, on the left a man and a woman are playing violas da gamba, on the right, the same, I hear nothing. I know the concert begins at eight, I feel imprisoned in the symmetry, I prepare myself to wait motionless for an hour, like a pillar devoted to art. But this idea is disturbed by a man in a black suit, the porter. He sees me standing there, opens the electronic door, and says: "You're either an hour early or you're part of it." I say: "I'm part of it."

I walk inside and go sit down in the first row, the music continues, they see me sitting there, I'm the only listener, I don't know anyone, but I know that the music transcends everything. When the piece ends, I take charge of the one-man applause and I shake hands with the ensemble. After this rehearsal with the singer, Claron McFadden, it is my turn. They want to hear my voice and see if I can stand up and sit down again on time. As *probatio pennae* I read a very short piece out loud:

RECEPTION

It was so warm that even my bare, dismantled intellect threatened to yield: the end of time. But on my way west it became overcast, and in Amsterdam it rained, I could breathe again. At the reception for Dagjos, on the grass of the Stadionkade, large trees and black umbrellas blocked the rain, the air cleared: the end of time had passed.

At eight o'clock every seat is occupied and The Spirit of Gambo begins the concert. *Consort Music of Four Parts* by the seventeenth-century English composer John Jenkins, compositions of about four minutes, alternating with readings of four minutes. The second part is music by Orlando Gibbons, sung by Claron McFadden. There is applause, the audience understands this music.

In the early evening I came 180 kilometers over a straight strip of concrete. In the late evening, I drive back over the same strip. In between, the gamba music, on instruments with carved animal heads. A symmetrical Saturday evening.

UKIYO-E

About the trip I took through Africa in 1957 in my father's old Land Rover, there are many things I could tell, but I'm limiting myself to ukiyo-e.

Each time I had to put the car on a raft or ferryboat, I was overcome by a strong feeling of futility. I wanted to end my journey, I did not want to go back home, that was not it, it was not homesickness, I wanted to end it, I wanted to switch off the car in my mind. There were always many people standing on the sandy shores, they were watching what came and went, but they were not traveling themselves. They were causing the feeling of dejection in my head. I wanted to watch the trip, I did not want to travel. In the vicinity of Dar es Salaam I spoke to a Japanese man who explained it to me. He said: "It is ukiyo-e."

MOLE

When the mole is there, I switch over into oracle-speak. I call him the king of darkness, friend of maggot, worm, and grub, traveler in the underworld, connoisseur of the soles of my feet. About that last, I have to laugh, he knows very well that my soles are above his head, but he can't see them, he can't be a connoisseur, he is blind. When a pyramid of earth appeared on my lawn for the first time, long ago, I ran wide-eyed and with open hands to my neighbor, the farmer, and cried out: The earth, neighbor! What's happening to the earth? My neighbor laughed, showed me the mole trap, and explained how I should position it. But I never did that, I turned out to have an innate reverence for the mole, master of the parallel world. I have never—and that is very difficult—seen a mole. Via language, certainly, I have certainly heard him described, but I have never seen him, in my life the mole is a creature that is never seen, like the crab that lives eight kilometers deep in the Indian Ocean and that no one has ever seen, not even my neighbor. I have adapted my view of the garden to the behavior of the mysterious, blind guest under the ground. Sometimes I stumble over a heavy tile in the garden path which has been tipped straight up like an iceberg in the night by the mole, but I don't curse, I have schooled myself in long suffering. The mole has probably come to symbolize, for me, what can never be understood—and what you therefore do not have to attempt to trap.

BOX

My youngest son has a girlfriend (could I also write *his girlfriend has my youngest son?*). They're going to have a child in November. My youngest son wants to put it in the same box he himself lay in, thirty-seven years ago. The box was nailed together by me and coated with primer. It was never painted. I look for the box in all the attics and in the hayloft and on the side platforms of the hayloft. I have four fully loaded barns, two made of wood, two of stone. I look everywhere, I can't find the box, the days are passing. This morning at eleven thirty, in the full sun, I go and look in the last uninspected place, in the locked, nearly impenetrable part of the second wooden barn, where I haven't been for years. I climb over boxes and shelving, and open the door. A frightened owl flies straight at me, dead quiet, as quiet as a shadow can fly, I look into his eyes—he's a large owl, it's not strange that I'm frightened too, we frighten each other. I myself thought that owls never moved in the daytime. What the owl thinks about me, I don't know.

FERAL CAT

For the last forty years I have had pets. I could give an enumeration, but I won't do that, I'll leave it to your imagination. Now I no longer have a single pet, but there are still many animals in the house and on the land—mice, titmice, foxes, rabbits, deer, owls. I see them sometimes, they see me, we have an understanding, but we are separate from one another, I don't feel responsible, and they have no obligation. So much for the tranquil, rural picture. Now comes the unrest, the mental rooting, the churning of the spirit, the abyss, the feeling of guilt, the feral cat. For years there has been a feral cat here in this area, I see it sometimes in the woods, but more often in the mown fields, it catches mice and birds, it is a pitiful, tough survivor. About a month ago I saw it with kittens, I must therefore say that I saw her with kittens. I remained strong and firm in my principles, but when I saw that there were fewer and fewer, I could no longer resist my feeling of guilt. I broke the code and every evening set a little container of food in the barn. Every morning it is empty.

SEVENTEENTH CENTURY

On my way to the Pieterskerk in Leiden I was passed on the highway by a sturdy van in camouflage colors. Not soldiers, idealists. On the bus was written *Seal Nursery*.

I thought of the letter that Frits Grönloh wrote from Middelburg on a Saturday afternoon at quarter past four on July 11, 1908, to his wife Agathe Tiket.

> This morning at two thirty I was already out with the Frenchman to take a hoogaars to sea in order to fish below Domburg. The Frenchman became so sick that at five thirty we had to turn back, then he fell asleep in the cabin.
>
> We took advantage of that to dry out on the sandbank for a moment on our way back and kick a small seal to death. The boat's Arnemuider captain lost no time hoisting him up by his hind feet and finished him off with his water boots before the creature was fully awake. This earns a 2.5-guilder bounty from the government. A little after seven thirty we were back at the jetty in Veere, the Frenchman was still half-dead from seasickness and cold and went straight to bed.

I was in the Pieterskerk for the first time in my life, I did not know what I was seeing, I had never seen anything so beautiful, I did not know that people could create anything so beautiful. I thought about the seventeenth century, and was secretly glad I was a Dutchman.

GENERATIVE GRAMMAR

In the beginning, when the house was still large and hollow and empty, it was often cold, too, for it had no stove. We would sit around the table wrapped in blankets, like Indians. In our family that was nothing special, but sudden visitors were surprised when we handed them a blanket. One such was my colleague Jan Zwart. He and I taught at the same high school, the same subject, Dutch linguistics and literature. It happened that he knew much more about it than I, so I often had to consult him. He knew a great deal not only about classical grammar, in which I could certainly still keep up with him, but also about Chomsky's generative grammar, which was completely above my head. When he sat thus unexpectedly wound in a blanket at the table with us, we had plenty to talk about. Yet he was not only above average in intelligence, he was also rigid and intransigent. When talking about his cherished beliefs, he would not back down. He was of the opinion that you didn't need to read anything else in the way of literature but the novels of Honoré de Balzac and Stendhal. When I proposed Couperus, Vestdijk, Mulisch, or Jan Wolkers, he would shake his head wearily: no, there's no need, I don't waste my time with them. It especially irritated me that he so belittled our own literature. But things went wrong between us through a misunderstanding, not through a profound conflict about Chomsky or Couperus.

I read aloud to him a poem that he did not know.

SUZANNE

Why didn't you die in Brussels?
I would have buried you in St. Joost ten Noode.
The horses would have trotted down from the hillside,
And on my knees lay tin flowers,
Which you can buy for 16 francs a wreath.
They stay purple for years, their stems are green, and
They come up again as soon as the snow melts.

This was our last contact, he offered no comment, he wanted nothing more to do with me, he systematically avoided me, he left me confused and amazed.

Much later, the rumors reached me. He had a wife named Suzanne, and he thought I was tastelessly joking with her name. I didn't even know that he had a wife, and further investigation revealed that she was not dead.

EGGS

I know someone who lives in the northernmost part of this country, in the mists of the Waddenzee. He lives in a little house that stands like a ship on the endless land, surrounded by the wind, which blows 360 days out of the year there—he has 5 days off. In the tidy living room is the bicycle that he made himself—a frame, a saddle, two wheels, two pedals, handlebars, a chain. No fenders, no brakes, no baggage carrier, no light, no chain guard, no gear lever, no bicycle bell. He cherishes the bicycle as a surgeon does his knives. I estimate that he is seventy years old. I like to tell this story to anyone who is willing to listen. Once a year I visit him. Yesterday, for example. I saw that the bicycle had a bell, I was disappointed. He explained to me that he was fined—twenty euros. The legislator requires a bicycle bell. He had taken eggs for his money.

FLAPSOUR

I have a woods in my backyard. It grew there by itself, it fell down out of the sky—seeds as propellers, seeds in parachutes of fluff, seeds in bird poop. I recognize the trees: beech, oak, ash, birch, chestnut, they are familiar brands—Opel, Volkswagen, Peugeot. But I recognize a Facel Vega only when someone says: "There goes a Facel Vega, a rare car."

In my woods stands one tree whose name I don't know, I call it "Flapsour's tree." It is the only tree that slants, slants very sharply, like a spear thrown from a great distance. I got it thirty years ago from a friend, who bought it at the Flapsour nursery in Drenthe.

In the summer, I often come to that part of my woods, I hang out the wash there, I have stretched the lines between the Opel, the Volkswagen, the Peugeot. There is also an iron chair, on which I lay the wet wash and on which I sometimes go and sit after working.

A few months ago something unusual happened, an inexplicable event.

I went with my wash to this woods, it was warm, good drying weather. On the iron chair a man was sitting reading a book. I asked him who he was, he said: "I'm Flapsour." I asked him what he was reading. He was reading "Poseidon," a story by Franz Kafka. The first sentences of the story: "Poseidon sat at his work-table doing calculations. The administration of all the waters gave him an endless amount of work." The story is shocking, Poseidon, who from the beginning of time has been appointed god of the sea, turns out to be an accountant, an administrator. While we think that with his trident he is traveling over the oceans of the world, he sits in the deep doing administrative work, he has never made a sea voyage. The last sentence of the story:

He was in the habit of saying that he was waiting for the world to perish, then there might well be a quiet moment for him in which, just before the end, after a review of the last calculation, he would still be able to go on a quick little tour.

This story made a great impression on me, so much so, in fact, that that evening, some time after Flapsour had left to return to Drenthe, I realized I had forgotten to ask him what kind of tree that was, which for thirty years, aslant like a spear, had been standing in my backyard.

SYNAGOGUE

Searching for a synagogue after midnight—I shouldn't have done it. Everything reverts back to "know yourself," an exhortation that is familiar to me, but that I often forget. I had given a reading in Loosbroek, a very small town in the neighborhood of 's-Hertogenbosch and Oss. I went there in the dark and I left in the dark, I saw only what my headlights saw, and that was not enough. In the church hall where I read for the Bernhezer Kunstkring, I asked which large town people here went to. Someone told me that Oss lay close by, but that he always said he lived in the vicinity of Den Bosch, because Oss had had a bad name from time immemorial. A splendid answer that you never hear in the light of the headlamps.

On my way home from Loosbroek, I went through Dieren, where two days later I was going to be reading in the synagogue, at Spoorstraat 34. I drove into Spoorstraat, a one-way street, but immediately I had passed 28 and saw 42. I was hallucinating, it was one thirty at night, I saw no one, everyone was asleep. I drove on and made a large loop through the city, because I did not want to give up. An essential fault, alien to my character—if I am really good at something, it is giving up. Perseverance is valued in our culture, by contrast, as the greatest virtue, perseverance is number one, God's Word and Commerce, never to give up, to persevere. Where was my insight into human behavior, why didn't I put myself in the place of the authorities? What would a policeman think when he saw a van driving slowly around and searching through a dead quiet Guelders city at one thirty at night? Out of the void, there they were behind me, I heard no trumpets, but saw two lights bright as the sun shining on me. The policeman came and stood next to me: engine off, window down. When he asked what I was doing, and I answered that I was looking for the synagogue, his suspicion closed tight like a net. He discovered that my driver's license had expired and went back to his cruiser, where he looked into my record, late rent payments, late alimony payments, outstanding fines, hash dealing, incitement to resist. This lasted a long time, but there was nothing improper to find out about me. He gave me back my papers, my wife went and sat behind the wheel and showed him her valid driver's license. By half past two, we were back home, I had trouble falling asleep, I felt I had been betrayed by myself.

ON THE REBOUND

I'm looking for an image for the new year. It will be a train, a loco-motive with separate cars, and a small, rural station (in England). I'm standing on the platform, fifteen minutes before midnight, I'm looking for a seat, we're riding into the new year, I don't know where the train will take me.

So much for the imaginary, now the reality. On Monday after-noon, New Year's Eve day, I'm tidying up my study, I find a letter from 1986 that I haven't yet answered. I calculate back, twenty-six years ago. When I write it this afternoon, it will be the first letter that I put in the mail in 2013. The writer was twenty-two years old in 1986, therefore he is now forty-eight. At that time he lived in Delft, at present he lives in Budapest. At that time he was poor, now he is rich, that is the way life must be—I love lives that ascend, though lives that go downhill seem to be more the intent of the Creator, the Creator is after all an artist, he wants misfortune, which means drama and tears and catharsis.

In 1986, the writer of the letter is friends with a young man named Sander who hasn't much money and eats out of trash cans, they know each other from the street.

The letter describes the only time that he visited Sander. On a winter's day he hears from other vagrants that it's his birthday. It's eleven o'clock at night, he prepares two little gifts (wrapped with ribbons and decorated with a paper peacock, comprising 1. Frankenstein's diary and 2. a book about Marilyn Monroe, with plenty of photos) plus a two-liter bottle of Lambrusco. At twelve o'clock he rings the doorbell, Sander opens it wearing two coats and two knitted caps. In the overcrowded room, in which the tem-perature hovers around freezing, a chair is cleared for him and the host pours the wine into glasses that he takes out of their original packaging, as a token of hospitality and trustworthiness. He tells a story about a friend who was left by his wife and *on the rebound* became a Jehovah's Witness.

The letter that I will send to Budapest on January 1 will be linguistic in nature. I will explain to him why *on the rebound* in this context is such a good choice.

MESSAGE

You seldom encounter Christians who say nothing about Jesus. That is logical, for his message is: Tell everyone, I am the Way, the Truth, and the Life. And Christians are not alone in having these claims, Muslims are also unfailingly convinced they are correct. As an atheist you can do no right.

Part of my family is vegetarian, I eat meat and must often pay for my bloodthirstiness with mockery. I have become accustomed to being taunted about this by Christians, Mohammedans, and vegetarians. But sometimes there is a chance for revenge.

I'm driving in the car with my vegetarians from Gorssel to Deventer. To the right, I see a cat coming out of the grass on the shoulder, mesmerized by his prey on the far side of the road. I see that he will suddenly accelerate—I know my animals—and will cross the road without any self-restraint. I honk the horn passionately for a long time, I wake him out of his trance, I save his life. The vegetarians haven't noticed anything. The Christians also don't notice that I love my neighbor, to say nothing of the Mohammedans. I myself say nothing about it, because I live without messages.

HELPLESS BECAUSE OF RESPECT

I used to have many animals (I could enumerate the kinds), at present I am animalless. There are people who claim that in your old age you may be comforted by a pet, but I believe that a pet just accentuates grief and loneliness. I miss my pigs the most— friendly, intelligent animals, tasty meat.

In 1993, Jaffe Vink asked me if I would answer ten difficult questions by Max Frisch for *Trouw*.

QUESTION 9
Would you rather be dead or live a while longer as a healthy animal? And which animal?

ANSWER
I would gladly prefer to live a while longer as a healthy pig. I have dogs, cats, chickens, turkeys, ducks, and a canary, and I'm rather attached to some of these animals. Most of all I like to be near my pigs, they smell so delectable and they sleep so delightfully. When I go look at them at night and listen to their gentle snuffling, I often feel like lying down next to them in the straw. I never do it, for fear of being regarded as crazy. I'm happy that Max Frisch has given me the opportunity to answer in all purity: a pig, please.

QUESTION 10
If, not of your own free will (like the holy Francis), but through circumstances, you were once again poor: would you then be just as tolerant as you used to be at the sight of the rich, now that, as one of them, you have gotten to know their way of thinking—helpless because of respect?

ANSWER
I would hate them. My day-to-day philosophy of resignation and asceticism is a thing of luxury based on abundance and well-being. Poor and needy in a moldy basement, I would hate the well-shod

legs of the people passing by. And perhaps I might also want to change something of my fate, for

Know thou, then, that thy voice by no one will be heard,
So long as thou prayest or beggest, stammering, at the gate.

BAT

I buy a heavy coal stove from a winegrower in France and transport it to Holland on a heavy trailer. There I build a chimney against the house that reaches above the ridge and in this way I heat the house for ten years. After that some reconstructions make the stove superfluous and the chimney must be taken down. If I fully extend the three-part ladder and stand on one of the highest rungs, if I then don't look down too often, my balance secured in a self-conceived but Zen Buddhist–derived manner—the stone chisel carefully in my left hand, the hammer in my right—I can break apart my construction stone by stone. But only if nothing goes wrong. I have laid an old mattress down below me, I want to keep the falling stones intact as much as possible. It is going well, sometimes a stone slips from under my chisel, falls on the roof, breaks a tile, but eventually lands where I intend it to, down below.

Yet an incident occurs after a short time of hacking. I am still standing very high up, well above the bravery limit. Out of a crack appears a living creature, we are eye to eye, I don't have much chance of dodging him. It's a bat. For an hour the little animal must have found itself in uncertainty and distress. Indeterminate violence, hellish noise, steel on steel. If I move, I will fall and be smashed, while he can move comfortably off on his wings. I stay still, I don't have the medieval fear of bats, he buzzes into the air past my face, I imagine that he touches my eyebrows, but it could also be the vibrating air. I watch him go, for a moment he continues to fly among the trees at my height. What is going to happen to him, is he blind, can he find a new shelter by day?

COMMON REDSTART

An hour before sunset, the unknown man came along on his bicycle, he greeted us over his shoulder, on his way to the woods. We were sitting outside, it was very warm, we greeted him in return. Twenty minutes later he was on his way back, he asked if we had a little box for the dragonfly that he held in the hollow of his fist. When the dragonfly was well stowed away, he gave a detailed, hour-long lecture on the dragonfly. I didn't have to say anything, I was thinking—not for the first time—that you can organize your life in whatever way you like. You can stand in front of people you don't know telling them everything about the dragonfly, not only its Latin name but also its Greek name, its evolution starting from prehistoric times, its natural habitat. I would not be able to do that, I would keep thinking: Do they really want to know this? Do they have time for it? Do they understand the words I'm using? But none of this troubled the man, he told us that at night he would regularly stand up to his shoulders in deep pools in the woods with a small camera in one hand and a very powerful lamp in the other. I asked if he wasn't ever afraid, but he did not understand my question, he said that these were very lonely places, there was never anyone there. The following day he returned, I was standing on the path, he showed me photos of rare dragonflies that recently existed only in Ingushetia in the Northern Caucasus, but now, as a result of climate change, could also be found in the Achterhoek. While he was talking, a common redstart was flying back and forth with little worms and little flies for its young, which have a nest in a crack in the wall of our house. The bird was torn between his fear of us and the urge to care for his young. That is why he kept going to sit for a moment on top of a stick that was supporting a dahlia. A good spot in which to be photographed. The third day the eccentric nature-lover had brought his large camera with him. When I got up, he was standing in front of the house in order to take photos, he was standing dead quiet, like a statue, his head hidden behind a lens like a cannon barrel. He stood there for a good hour, now and then I looked out of the house at him, he did not see me, he saw only the redstart.

SOUP BOWL

"Bake bread" is the first thing my grandson calls out when I meet him on the path. He has made a long journey, I lift him up, and my plan is to talk a little about a poem by Ezra Pound, in order to sway his thoughts. He is just four years old, but with poetry you can't begin too early.

In the house he immediately hauls his little step stool over to the kitchen counter, where I turn the flour, the water, and the yeast in the mixing bowl of the electric mixer. This is his moment, he is fascinated by the revolving of the dough hook. And this is where the danger lurks, if the oven timer no longer works and the television no longer goes on, to say nothing of the computer, you know that his love of button technology is boundless. But the electric mixer belongs to another age, that of heavy industry, the Soviet Union, the Cold War, repetitive motions, indifferent disasters. My grandson on the low step stool—I can't let him out of my sight for a second, I am not a relaxed cook, I am a grim watchman who does not belong in the kitchen.

But an accident does happen, not with the dough hook, the machine is quiet, the dough is rising under a damp cloth, there is no direct danger. We are standing by another counter, he has moved the step stool, I'm spreading a slice of bread, I'm standing with my back to him, I hear something unusual, I turn around and see him fall from the step stool, his arms are waving and he hits a soup bowl. When he strikes the floor in a sitting position nothing much is wrong, but the soup bowl follows him down and lands right on his head. Alarm, bump, and tears, moderate, the unrestrained grief explodes only once I have taken him to his mother, comforting is her job, he knows that. I weigh the soup bowl, six hundred grams.

STORY

Everything has its story. The edge of the woods, which after a light snowfall becomes transparent and comprehensible. The country road that has been tamed by a double line down the center. The poultry, beleaguered by swiftly swerving birds of prey. The pleasure of letting the chicken feed run through your fingers. The cultured man in the train who furtively drinks wine out of the bottle, good wine from the looks of it. Children who are just beginning their lives. The car that has trouble starting in the cold. The house entered by soldiers in the night.

My seven-year-old daughter comes and stands by our bed and whispers that there are men walking through the house. I get up, do not turn on any lights, I listen. I hear voices outside on the path, it is pitch black, you can't see your hand in front of your eyes. I join the group, they are soldiers, I am the hand in front of their eyes. Then we hear the scouts come out of the house, they say to the commander: "We can sleep here, the shack is uninhabited." This happened forty years ago.

Yesterday, my eight-year-old granddaughter stayed here. She told me that she had had a horrible night. She had dreamed that murderers were walking through the house, but luckily I had chased them away, I still play a role in her life. She doesn't know the story about the soldiers, the house has preserved it for her and cast it in the form of a dream.

THE MAIN DISH

The neighborhood where sex was the main dish was at its most
lovely in the mornings at sunrise. The dairy farmer clattered his
cans, the baker smoked a cigarette on the front steps while he
gazed at the wood pigeon in the gutter of the brothel across from
his store. In winter, very early, I rode my bicycle to the Haarlemmerdijk, where, in the cellars of a Roman Catholic girls' school,
I filled two large stoves with coke so that at nine o'clock the girls
could go stand in a warm classroom against the central heat-
ing. Sometimes, when the cold was too severe, the headmistress
would telephone me at the end of the morning and order me to
come stoke the fires a little more. When I was in Haarlem, where
I sat with white gloves on leafing through incunabula, she could
not reach me, but when I was at home explaining to Impala Appie
that in jij *wordt* the t must be written down even though you don't
hear it, and in *word* jij it must be omitted even though there, too,
you don't hear it, I was a helpless prey to the headmistress. Impala
Appie would then drive me to the Haarlemmerdijk in his Chevro-
let Impala convertible. In the summer he always drove with the
roof folded down, that's why he had bought it—in order to show
his girl to the neighborhood. I stoked the fires only in winter and
thus never sat in the open car, I was a bird that wintered over. Appie could not imagine that I did this heavy and unhealthy work of
stoking in exchange for a mere gratuity and asked why I did not,
like him, put a girl in the window, my house was very well suited
for that, I lived in the right neighborhood and it brought in much
more than stoking.

I helped him with Dutch because he was studying for his small-
business license. He wanted to buy a hairdressing business for
his girl. I don't know if anything ever came of it, because I left the
neighborhood and went to live in a forest.

My relationship with Impala Appie was not such that I could

broach the inner aspects of pimping. I mean the question of whether it did not strike him as difficult to share his loved one with so many others. Jealousy does, after all, sit in the front seat alongside love, or in his case was economic gain the ultimate boss? If we had become friends I could have put this question to him sometime and perhaps I could also have asked him something about the mystery that later preoccupied me. It concerned a friendly, serious girl who also earned her money in sin. I talked to her once and knew that she was saving up for a little house in the country. Chickens and an apple tree—that's what she was dreaming of. When I hadn't seen her for a few weeks, the rumors reached me. Her pimp, who did not live with her, had in her absence broken open the cupboard and found her savings, sixty thousand guilders. In a single night gambled away.

Considerable time went by before she resumed her place, she was starting over again. Even the pimp was pointed out again. I knew him, we greeted each other, I felt like saying "you dirty bastard" to him, but my limited talent for martial arts stopped me.

CONTAINER

On the highway from Rotterdam to Vladivostok, on the train through the Betuwe, on the ships on the Twentekanaal, everywhere, I see the containers that hold our earthly possessions. Last week I sat in that sort of locked container for eight hours. Not alone, I was in the company of Joubert Pignon, a young writer who works in a pet shop, and he in turn was in my company. We were invited to the Noorderzon Festival in Groningen, we were reading aloud.

We sat next to each other on a comfortable leather sofa, the audience sat on wooden benches, twenty-five people, always more women than men, in one case twenty-four women and one man. When the herring were assembled in the barrel, the organizer shut the steel doors from outside. Anyone who has ever had a close look at a container knows that the sealing mechanism is calculated for transporting elephants. There were no ventilation ducts, there was no air-conditioning, there were no windows. We read alternately, very short stories, Joubert's were on average somewhat longer than mine. The agreement was that after twenty minutes the organizer would bang on the outside of our housing with a piece of wood and open the doors. He did this punctually, fortunately, for after twenty minutes the oxygen was used up—the healthy life whizzed inside and caused a feeling of rescue, escape, release. After ten minutes we went back inside and the doors were shut. The organizer had announced the event as a marathon, but I had more the idea of a hurdle race. After it was over, it seemed that Joubert Pignon had taken the hurdles more easily than I had. Not only because he is much younger than I am and thus can do with less oxygen than I, but most of all because he works in a pet shop, where you are close to nature and thus used to the ever-present danger.

THE BAKER'S WIFE

When you write a very short story every day, you have to think of an opening sentence 365 times a year. As far as that's concerned, you'd do better to be a novelist, one or two opening sentences a year. This morning I wanted to write something about the baker's wife, but she didn't want that, I couldn't get the first sentence down on paper. In such cases a little bike ride sometimes helps. It was half past seven, the day promised to be beautiful, although the sun had not yet shown itself. Hanging over the land were rags of mist that in this area are called *witte wieven* (white-women spirits), beautiful and cold. After a few kilometers my hands and ears were getting cold— cap and gloves forgotten, still too much summer in my head.

I cycled past the little bench where I sometimes go and sit. Although it is in a quiet place outside of town, it is nicely painted and bears scarcely any marks of boredom or destructiveness. It was donated by the owner of the local driving school in 2003, the town council chose the spot. A few months ago I saw that it was being painted. I stopped to thank the town employee for his ongoing care, especially in this time of crisis and shortage of funds, but when I saw the advertisement on the car I realized that the owner of the driving school himself was the one maintaining his gift. Later, on my way back, there was even a little sign with *Wet* on it. Since then, when I ride there I always have ideas about the meaning of community, as I am having now, once again. They are vague ideas about the role of the government and the duty of citizens. These ideas change to surprise when I ride past the golf course, where two ladies are hitting a little ball in a patch of mist this morning before eight o'clock. I had a completely different idea about golfers. Especially because I occasionally see that a boy walks with them carrying the equipment.

The result of my little ten-kilometer bike ride was that I forgot about the baker's wife, but I realized it only this afternoon when I bought a loaf of bread.

LITTLE BOX

When yesterday's letter fell into the mailbox, the dragonfly man and I stayed and talked a little longer. He told me that he had once, as a goldsmith, for a wager, made a very small box with a hinged lid, a cube measuring one millimeter. I could not believe my ears, but I had heard it all the same, he would bring it with him on his next visit. Bicycling home, I mumbled "that can't be that can't be that can't be," but on the other hand I have never caught the dragonfly man lying. There is a chance that this story will have a sequel.

The dragonfly man has come to visit with his little box and a very powerful magnifying glass. I saw it, one by one by one millimeter including lid and hinge. An insurmountable philosophical problem has now arisen: my eyes have not relayed an enduring signal to my brain. Out of eye, out of brain—I can't contain it, he will have to come back with the little box, the wonder will have to be constantly renewed. The little box has transformed me into a believer.

FORTY CENTIMETERS

At Blokker's, I have bought a handy metal lantern that gives a lot of light. I have hung it from a nail in the room, and I try to remember where the nail is, so that I will have light when the electric current fails. Sometimes in the evening when it is dark, I take the lantern out with me to the chicken coop to see if my worries are warranted. In the coop live a small rooster, a small hen, and two very small chicks. The hen sits in a corner on the ground, the chicks can't be seen, they are sitting under the hen.

The rooster sleeps on a shelf, forty centimeters higher up. That was where the hen sat, too, before the birth of the chicks. I dread the moment when the hen will go sleep next to the rooster again, and the chicks will remain behind on the ground and die in the cold of the night. One evening, I see in the light of the lantern from Blokker's that the hen is sitting next to the rooster again. I shine the light over the floor but I don't see any chicks. I continue to look until a chick sticks its little head out from under its mother. They are still extremely small and have hardly any wings, I don't understand how they have managed to get up those forty centimeters. I attribute it to life instinct, whatever that may be. During the day I also look at the chickens. Then I scatter their feed and see that the chicks learn from their mother what they must pick up, and how.

Gerrit Krol writes in his essay "The Brief Life of our Understanding":

> The problem has a scientific counterpart in the question of whether the pecking behavior of a chick is learned or innate. Innate, says one half of science, because it pecks while still in the egg. Even in the egg, says the other half, you can learn something. Scientifically speaking—meaning in hindsight, logically reasoned—both views are correct.

Because I have no talent for science, I am always very happy with these last four words: *both views are correct.*

THE PAST

On the day that it is thirty degrees in the shade, the motorcycle comes driving up the path. Not obtrusive and insolent, which, after all, is the nature of a motorcycle, but, on the contrary, hesitant and thoughtful. I stand there waiting, the driver stops thirty meters away and sets the machine carefully on its stand. It is a beautiful thing, a well-maintained field motorcycle in cheerful colors, green, yellow, and blue, I feel hopeful again and walk slowly over to it. The man is dressed for summer, in a shirt and shorts, he is rummaging around a bit in a saddlebag, takes out a little book of maps and leafs through it. He is wearing a helmet and sunglasses. I say: "From your behavior I can tell that you know me, but I can't trust that this is mutual; even if you were at the door only yesterday, that is no guarantee that I would recognize you today."

He says something in answer while, without haste, he removes his helmet and sunglasses. He mumbles: "I have something for you, but I can't find it . . . okay, here it is." It is a photo from September 1991, black-and-white, in it I'm standing with a very large dog at my side, which strikes me all the more because I was thinner in 1991 than at present. Now I also know who the man is, he brought the dog with him to the job, because he was in the process of getting a divorce. When the work was finished, he asked if the animal could stay with us. I said no, I already had two dogs. He sighed and said that in that case the animal would be taken to the vet's for an injection. That seemed to me unfair, and therefore I said yes. We had him for years, he was a good-natured dog, his name was Bennie, he was afraid of thunderstorms, but died a natural death.

Now, twenty-one years later, I ask his master if he really meant that, about the injection. He laughs and says that he suspected I was a sentimental man, on whom that sort of disguised threat would be effective. A good answer, I like it when a carpenter understands human nature.

CHRISTMAS PRESENT

The Twentekanaal empties into the IJssel via a lock. I often stand there looking at the ships that go up and down in an elevator of water. The construction is beautiful, the ships seem to be indestructible, yet never far away is the thought of ukiyo-e, the fleeting nature of reality, a concept belonging to Japanese Buddhism.

One December years ago I had a conversation there with a ship's captain who had just passed through the lock but was not going on. He was standing on the wall next to the moored ship and gazing at the great expanse of sky above the river. I said "ukiyo-e." He said: "Yes, I can't help thinking of that, too, come inside, we'll have something to drink." He looked like my father, so I followed him over the gangplank. He had been traveling on the cutter for thirty years by now, he no longer had a house. There were three dogs on board, the youngest was lively and restless. No dog for a ship, a dog for the fields, long, supple motions in pursuit of wild animals. He asked if I wouldn't take the dog, as a Christmas present. I didn't want him, I already had two dogs, five cats, chickens, ducks, guinea hens (never counted), three geese, and a small horse. But the words "Christmas present" weakened me, awakened my Christian charity, I took the dog home with me. In our place, too, he remained a stranger, went unbidden after wild animals, indeed once bit one of our own chickens to death, was surly toward the cats and behaved arrogantly toward the other dogs.

The forest warden came by to listen to the tone of my words. He could hear if I was guilty of the dog's behavior. He came three times to determine this—he did not consider me guilty, but advised me to get rid of the dog. Two years went by before I saw the cutter by the lock again, and happily it was December once again. "I've come to bring back the Christmas present," I said. The ship's captain looked at me thoughtfully, with eyes half-shut. "Let's take care of it in turns," he said. This meant that the dog, who meanwhile had been named Ukiyo-e by the captain as well as by me, would change its home with a regularity determined by chance. And this was done, the Christmas present has in the meantime moved four times—water and land, ebb and flood, day and night.

IN LOUTH

I wrote: I was thinking about the war that did not break out. Then I receive a message from England from a friend. He writes:

In Louth there is a church. In the church is a little kitchen booth and in that booth is a little old woman. She is just now cleaning up, her taxi is already on its way, but there is still time for a slice of cake. When she hears where I'm from, she tells me that she has been in Nijmegen. Her brother is buried there. You go there for your brother, she says, and once you're there and see all those other graves, you feel that you're not the only one who has lost someone. She was a year older than he in 1944. He was then 21. I calculate quickly and conclude that she is about 90.

A BRUTE, A LITTLE TREASURE

Early in the morning I receive the message from Branko V., in Hotel Hampshire, in Groningen. I had read there for two days with Joubert Pignon inside a ship's container at the Noorderzon Festival. Branko writes that he wants to buy Lucy:

> A little tugboat thirteen meters long, apparently a real workboat, black and dark gray, the deck red, the cabin made of teak, and a Hiab crane. A brute, a little treasure. She's trying to seduce me.

He travels to Brabant, where Lucy is moored. The woman he meets there asks him: "What sort of interest do you have in this? Is it really serious?" Later, on the boat, she adds: "Do you really have the money? I have no intention of spending a lot of time on someone who isn't going to buy the boat."

Early in the morning I walk out of the hotel. After ten steps I am standing on the Winschoten quay, I'm looking at Ooster harbor, where, right in front of me, a small tug is manoeuvering a houseboat. A tug of about thirteen meters, a brute, a little treasure. A wispy cloud hangs above the harbor, the sun has no problem with it. On this morning, so full of expectancy, everyone has been thinking about the meaning of life, no one has gotten a satisfactory answer, except those who are self-satisfied or empty.

EVA

Over the IJsseldijk cars drive toward Zwolle and toward Deventer. In the vicinity of Olst, they drive without noticing over the inlet dating from the Cold War, almost no one, still, knows anything about it: the plan that the water would be dammed with half-submerged pontoons and flowing through the secretly constructed inlets, after fourteen days the valley lying under water. Hundreds of thousands of people abandoning their houses, including Eva Kupfernick, who in the thirties came to our country as a German servant girl and since then has lived in Twello. During the war things are difficult for her, it is rumored that she belongs to the fifth column, but she survives because her mistress passionately defends her and guarantees her political innocence. Later she marries a retired biologist. At the wedding ceremony she conducts herself in accordance with an old German custom as a young, virginal girl. Her old mother has made a linen handkerchief for her and hands it to her on the morning of the celebration. The bride holds the handkerchief in her hand during the ceremony and dries her tears with it. Before the wedding night it is laid unwashed and soaked in tears in the linen cupboard and is taken from it again only when the woman is lying on her deathbed. Then her frozen features are covered with the handkerchief, which in the end accompanies her into the grave. Eva Kupfernick will reach the age of eighty-six and has never known that she would have had to leave her house if the water had been used to protect the country against invaders from the east.

TOWN LINE

Jan is struck by Piet. This sentence is in the passive form. Grammatically, Jan is the subject, but emotionally he is the direct object, the suffering object, he will, after all, be struck. I liked to talk about this when I was a teacher. I also liked to talk about the first page of *Villa des Roses* by Willem Elsschot. On that page there was a sentence that I had cherished since my youth:

> Under the circumstances, only the grass was able to endure, grass
> which thrives all the more luxuriantly the less it is tended and which
> is a friend of forgotten stones and buildings falling into ruin.

I taught: if anyone happened to read this book, he should pay attention to the last two sentences, then he would immediately, and forever, know what writing meant.

On my third peg hung Anthonis de Roovere, a Flemish poet of the fifteenth century. The pupils had to learn his *Van der Mollenfeeste* by heart. By heart! I was very strict about this, I wanted them to give a close reading to one vanitas poem so that Nicolaas Matsier would not later write in the newspaper that "they no longer know anything." Parents protested in vain to the headmaster, and when after some time I was dismissed, it was not on account of the vanitas poem, but owing to a bureaucratic rule unknown to me: last in, first out.

This was almost thirty years ago, the economy was not flourishing, there were many unemployed, I was one of them. I had a benefit that was not permanent, and a house of my own. To my horror there was also a rule that after some time I would have to consume that house. Information officials used this term without laughing. I did not laugh either, I had worries and sleepless nights. What I did laugh about were the forms. These said that I would have to report to the authorities if I crossed the town line, because "I had to be available to the labor market." I wrote letters of application and was often invited for an interview. Always at Catholic schools, because I read the help wanted ads in *de Volkskrant*, a newspaper that was no longer officially Catholic and indeed employed pagan journalists, but with a constituency that could not forget the taste of those little wafers, the fragrance of the incense, and the murmur of the chaplain in the confessional. During the interview I would talk about the passive sentence, *Villa des Roses*, and Anthonis de Roovere, but I never neglected to give my opinion about Catholicism (my mother always insisted that I never lie). I was never hired.

Before I crossed the town line, I would call the city official on duty to let him know. After the second time, the man said that no one did that and I should not do it either. But I continued to do it because the form demanded it, I wanted to remain honest. This went on for a few years, the meal with the house on my plate was approaching. Some weeks before I would have to take the first bite, I received a message from the employment office. I should apply to a public police school. There, no one cared what I thought about Catholicism, I was hired. Remained till time for my pension, house intact.

ACCOUNTANT

I walk through the floodplains of the IJssel looking for my glass eye, which has fallen out of its socket. I find the eye and see the old man who is always thinking about camel drivers in Outer Mongolia and silkworms in the Chinese Empire. Standing eye to eye with him, I ask him if he is a dream. He nods. I ask him what a dream is. He says: "That you think you can see me with your glass eye." I ask: "Am I dreaming you right now?" He says: "Yes, at this moment I'm sitting in my accounting office in Deventer—you do know I'm an accountant, don't you?"

CORK OAK

When the roosters crow in the distance I want to go off on a journey. Nearby, they don't have that effect. My chicken coop is far away from the house, at this time of year the crowing begins between six and six thirty. When I'm asleep I am not woken up by it, but when I'm awake I can't go back to sleep because of it. The words cork oak also awaken my wanderlust—the crowing and the cork oak, those are the culprits.

I have a friend who in the sixties lived as a hermit. When his summer vacation began—at five o'clock in the afternoon of his last workday in the office—he immediately drove off to Barcelona. He had an old Citroën Deux Chevaux that did not go fast, but this didn't matter to him, his habit was to drive straight through, day and night, he stopped only to fill the tank and buy a bar of chocolate. In Barcelona he would park his car by the harbor, pick up his diving gear, and take a boat to an island where he went every year. He would sleep out in the open on a little beach between inaccessible rocks, reachable only via a long and dangerous footpath. He never spoke to anyone, no other person had been in that place since prehistoric times. He stayed as long as possible, he calculated it very precisely, the walk, the boat trip back to Barcelona, the uninterrupted drive back to Amsterdam, the stops for filling the tank and the chocolate bars, and finally the arrival at the office at eight o'clock in the morning, when his first workday, till five o'clock, began. One detail that I have saved for last is this.

He did not dive in order to look at beautiful, graceful fish, he dove to visit desolate underwater caves. Often, their entrances were so narrow that he had to take his oxygen tank off his back and pull it in after him.

If something had gone wrong, he would have remained till the end of time undiscovered. That is certainly something quite different from daydreaming at the crowing of a rooster and mooning over the words cork oak.

THE SWANS

About the swans, there is this to say: There are three, they are always together, but they have a secret, two are inseparable, one must keep his distance, and he does that. They are very shy, they sit in quiet places in the meadow or swim in quiet water—they disappear as soon as they see me. Sometimes, when they fly low over the land, no higher than five meters, I see them from very nearby. Now the roles are reversed, they seem not to notice me and I in turn walk with my head between my shoulders. These are rustling airplanes, much larger than on the ground, through the surrounding air of another dimension.

On a stormy autumn night I once saw three swans swimming one after the other in a small, narrow canal in Amsterdam. I got out of my car and felt compassion for them, there was not much space, the bridges lay so close to one another that the swans could no longer raise themselves up out of the water, they were doomed to remain city swans forever. When I returned to that spot a couple of hours later to retrieve the car, I saw, in the same place in the water, three men in canoes in a strict line one behind the other. They were soldiers on some unknown mission, they were wearing helmets with headlamps. They were not invented, they belonged to the reality of the night. In fact, there is nothing to invent, there were armored police cars everywhere, with agents and their shields. They were protecting the city from Scottish soccer fans. I sat still, I couldn't start the car, I did not know how to do it anymore. I squeezed my hands, I tried to think of my Amsterdam driving instructor from 1955, how do you start a car? But I did not succeed, it was the Scots, the agents' shields, the soldiers in their canoes, and of course the swans. I waited until morning, I slept now and then, leaning against the car door. When it grew light, I woke up, my head was clear again, I started the car and drove to the shore at Bloemendaal. At Parnassia I walked down to see the swans, but they weren't there. I consulted a blonde woman who was out with her German shepherd—she said she had never seen swans on that shore, though she had lived her whole life on the coast.

1) In the fields around our house a flock of ± 100 sheep has appeared. The shepherd drives an all-terrain vehicle and wears a broad-brimmed leather hat. The fields are not fenced in, there is a drainage ditch and there are edges of woods. The shepherd marks out a large pasture with light material, connected with a battery. The sheep eat a lot, he must move the pasture after three or four days. At this time the flock runs free, guarded by two dogs. I live in a world most of whose phenomena I don't understand— mobile telephones, the gear hub on my bicycle, Skype, the war in Syria. But the enigma of the two dogs that keep the flock of sheep together surpasses everything. Through the kitchen window, I watch how they do it, I am by myself, I can't tell anyone what I'm seeing.

2) On Christmas Day I see that my youngest son, in the distance, is being accosted by a passing man. Amsterdam, Frederik Hendrikstraat, a tram pauses next to the stop across from Albert Heijn.

Later I hear from my son what the stranger said: "You do know, don't you, that the President of Syria himself caused the civil war?"

3) Jules Renard writes on August 22, 1909, in his journal: "The truth always dims our splendor. Art exists in order to falsify the truth."

4) On October 4, he writes: "The truth exists only in the imagination. Choice in truth lies in observation. A poet is an observer who immediately recreates. The proof is that, when next he looks at people, he does not recognize them."

5) The fencing now stands close to the house, eight meters from the kitchen window. The shepherd and the dogs have left, I'm

making coffee, the sheep see that I'm busy. Too bad Martinus Nijhoff is dead, coffee and sheep, he could have made something out of that.

AFRICA

The mayor of Lochem has stepped down from his post. He has a dream, he wants to return to teaching dyslexics. He asks if I will keep my speech very short.

The dream is not a goal, a finishing line, applause, profit. The dream is not about exertion, four thousand hours of work has already been done on it. For a dream, slaps on the back are superfluous, a bonus unknown. The dream is a migratory bird. In the solitary house in the delta someone is standing at the window, he is looking at the migratory birds, he tells no one. In Africa someone is waiting for the birds, he doesn't talk about it, he doesn't even have to see them.

A WOMAN

Above the path in the woods behind my house where I walk every day I see a buzzard flying among the great beeches. In brief segments, ahead of me, from tree to tree, he keeps in touch with me. At the same time I see a woman in the distance, which is remarkable because almost never does anyone walk here. The woman and the buzzard are connected through my gaze. About the buzzard I know nothing, except that Icarus also tried it: flying. He succeeded, but he knew no measure, he came too close to the sun, the wax of his wings melted, he plummeted into the sea, a white leg was the last we saw of him. The buzzard does not know the mystery of flying, he flies without knowing it. I think of him and because of my thoughts he exists.

With the woman it is different, she is a person, I know her possibilities and limitations, they are the same as mine. I nod, she stands still and asks me a question about the way to Almen, she asks how long she can go on walking in the woods. I think of Till Eulenspiegel, who replied to such a question only when he knew how fast the wanderer was walking. I have small-scale thoughts, I assume that just like me she has had breakfast, drunk coffee, read the paper with outrage—injustice, war, rising water. But I'm mistaken, she isn't going for a walk, she is doing a tour on foot, she has been on the road for forty days, she is walking from Lodz in Poland to Amsterdam, eleven hundred kilometers. It is a project, she is an artist, her actions cannot be measured. Although I am speechless, I say that it is four kilometers to Almen, perhaps five.

NO SMOKING

Last night I gave a reading at the largest airfield that the Germans constructed in occupied territory (at that time Holland was already one of the first). They hid their airplanes in buildings disguised as farms with painted roof tiles and painted windows with Dutch curtains on walls painted to resemble bricks. This airfield still exists in 2013, in the hangars you can read that you may not smoke, *Rauchen Verboten*, you must still know German. I read in a gigantic hangar heated by a machine that stood outside in the pouring rain and blew its heat inside through a proboscis wrapped in blankets. There were twenty people present (counting quickly). The organizer had pushed a pair of long tables together and there we sat cozily side by side. If there had been, among the visitors, a woman who clearly hated me and with a white, contorted face called out every fifteen minutes that I could not write and that I had unjustly encroached upon the terrain of literature, the evening would have been spoiled for me. But this woman was among the absent, I had a pleasant evening and at eleven o'clock drove home contented through the dark woods.

BEGINNING & END

I confused the beginning with the end. Then I made a mistake in the erratum. Finally the erratum fled into the universe of the internet and I stood there empty-handed.

All I can do now is leave the arithmetic to others. I must confine myself to the facts: the Great War lasted from '14 to '18, the Belgians supplied the battlefields, the Dutch remained neutral.

OH MY BRIDE

In December 1998, I was watching *Dead Poets' Almanac*, Sunday evening, VPRO, and saw Stevie Smith read a poem. I was very impressed and thought: Oh, what a poem. The poet was unfamiliar to me, I had never heard her name. I don't know who I should blame for that. It reinforced in me a thought that I often entertain: What does the parallel world look like—how small is the official world, what will be remembered of me?

I REMEMBER
It was my bridal night I remember,
An old man of seventy-three
I lay with my young bride in my arms,
A girl with t.b.
It was wartime, and overhead
The Germans were making a particularly heavy raid on Hampstead.
What rendered the confusion worse, perversely
Our bombers had chosen that moment to set out for Germany.
Harry, do they ever collide?
I do not think it has ever happened,
Oh my bride, my bride.

The whole poem was obscure to me because there was one word I didn't understand: *temee*. I mumbled it a good thirty-four times per hour and noticed that it came swimming up from my past. It was an ordinary word from the world of my grandma, who was born in the nineteenth century on Lindengracht in Amsterdam. After a few days of thinking about it, I remembered the meaning: *immediately*. *Van Dale* says: *instantly, soon, right away*. But also: *just a moment ago*.

I believe my grandma's father was a carpenter. He certainly could not have been a professor. They did not live in the Jordaan at that time. Those who wanted to better themselves left the neighborhood. My grandma did that by marrying a well-to-do printer/publisher. In my time they lived in Van Baerlestraat. I slept at their place once, on the sofa in the living room. On the wall hung a small tile: *To improve the world, begin with yourself.*

FRISIANS

An Italian meal with a Scottish drummer in the city of Groningen. He orders a Sardinian dish and talks with the owner, who was born in Sardinia and goes back eight times a year to his island, his parents, his friends, his youth. The Scottish drummer has lived in Amsterdam for a long time by now and speaks Dutch. When he doesn't know a word he has recourse to the Scots, as a result of which there arises a language which strict grammarians would scorn but which to my great pleasure they can't prevent.

I recount something about language. I'm standing in a Frisian elevator. It goes up and down in the retirement community where my parents live. I'm not alone, two ladies are there with me, their combined ages not less than 160 years. There is some confusion over how to work the elevator buttons. One of the ladies tells me a story, but I understand none of it. There is no reason to be snippy and so I say quite neutrally: "I don't understand you, I'm Dutch." She says: "We're in Friesland here." I say: "Yes, I know, but you speak Frisian and Dutch, and I understand only Dutch, so in this case the choice does not seem difficult to me." She says: "The Dutch are always trying to dominate us." I say: "I'm not trying to dominate you, I want to talk to you in a language we both understand." And because I want to give a little spice to my tame attitude, I add: "Besides, Dutch is the main language in this country." Whereupon she concludes this little dialogue with the words: "But the Frisians were here first." With that, she surprises me. Were the Frisians in this country before the Limburgers, the Amsterdammers, the Jews, and the Turks? I'll have to check this. As she leaves the elevator, she says sharply: "Goodbye, Mister Dutchman." The remaining Frisian woman says quietly: "There are Frisians and there are Frisians."

THE SHEEP

For four days now the sheep have been eight meters from my house, almost a hundred animals, a few with bells around their necks. They don't keep me from sleeping, but if I can't sleep I hear their magical tinkling far away in the night. This morning, the shepherd is busy setting up the enclosure, I go out and speak to him for the first time, I am especially interested in the dogs, but we also talk about the power of the electricity in the wires and about the beetles. The sheep graze the whole day, their dung is drawn down into the earth and spread through it by beetles, in the spring it is available for the new grass. Farmer and shepherd both profit—man, sheep, dog, beetle.

While we are talking the flock runs free, far away from us by the edge of the woods. The older dog, an experienced border collie, lies in the grass and watches the flock tensely, he fetches personally each sheep that threatens to wander off. The other dog is young, runs restlessly back and forth. The shepherd answers my questions, sometimes gives him an instruction, keeps an eye on the flock in the distance, pulls the fencing out of the ground, and makes me feel I am a useless and superfluous person—a good feeling. The young dog is a cross between a border collie and a shepherd. "There's more shepherd in him," says the shepherd. That means he is more suited for maintaining lines. That will now be taught to him. The shepherd makes a motion as though he is setting out a line a hundred meters long, the dog must understand that he should maintain the invisible limit for the flock. He must understand all the gestures that in one motion indicate all the imaginary limits within which the sheep must stay. This he can learn, he is capable of it. He must also not be too nippy, but also no softy, for a sheep can be a determined runaway, and then it is very handy if the dog can wrestle him down to the ground and keep him under control. The dog is wild and at the same time obedient, he immediately stops eating the sheep shit when his master orders him to. "Otherwise he vomits in the car later on," he says. I want to know a few more little things, but he has to leave, his day is overfilled with work. I go back into the house, I go and sit down at a bare table.

OWL

During the past week, at night, an owl has been flying over the house. He shrieks in order to frighten his prey—perhaps he has his eye on me as well. If this were Shakespeare's England, I would be frightened because in those times the cry of an owl in the night was an announcement of death. But those times are past, now what I have to be afraid of is that someone will enter my head via my computer and read my thoughts. Here, superstition has made no advances. Concerning the owl, by the way, I read a line by the Polish poet Wisława Szymborska: "In certain circumstances the owl is the baker's daughter." And when I hear the nocturnal cries I have to laugh a little about the baker's daughter. In the poem the queens Mary Stuart and Elizabeth Tudor were also named, in fact—it should not surprise me that Shakespeare lived at the same time.

Yesterday toward sunset I stood by the lock in Eefde, where the Twentekanaal comes out into the IJssel. Another man also stood there watching, wearing a long, white fur coat, a polar bear in summer. I actually see him often, we don't speak to each other, but nod by way of sealing the peace. I don't want to say anything about that fur coat, but on the back of it from top to bottom a fiery red ribbon has been sewn, ten centimeters wide. And that is the reason I don't feel entirely comfortable. I deem it not out of the question that it isn't the owl shrieking by my house at night, but this man with his fur coat and that red ribbon.

SUCKLING PIG

I often think about a photo that I've never seen. It was taken on New Year's Eve in 1926 in Yugoslavia. A man in a tuxedo is enjoying himself in a nightclub with two beautiful women in low-cut evening dresses. Under his arm he is holding a suckling pig. The women are laughing and so is he, the pig is not laughing, it is holding its mouth wide open, it is probably squealing.

Now that I write it down, I realize that this is an expression: "to squeal like a pig." And I also realize that I never hear this expression anymore. The boy next door to us was often struck by his father, the walls were thin, at these times my mother would say: "He's squealing like a pig again." There was no television, she did not yet know which authority she should notify. Time slips away and takes language with it. The man in the tuxedo would become, in 1938, the father of the poet Charles Simic. He had acquired the pig through his dexterity. At midnight the lights went out, and to celebrate the new year a suckling pig was released. In the rising chaos as the year 1926 turned into 1927, he was able to capture the little creature. The lights went on again, he was congratulated and got a piece of rope which he tied around the pig's foot. After that, the party went on till daybreak and ended in a nondescript bar where a drunken priest was uniting a young pair of lovers in matrimony. He crossed a knife and a fork to bless them. Charles Simic's father gave them the little pig as a wedding present.

When I owned pigs, it could also happen once in a while that I spent the night sitting in the barn when piglets were being born. The wind rustled in the poplars and the owl hooted. A great contrast with the man celebrating in his Yugoslavian tuxedo. In my life almost nothing has happened, but I don't know if I should be sorry about that.

CRIME PASSIONNEL

The man who comes uninvited to sit at my little table in the train station restaurant immediately begins talking about Alceo Dossena (1878–1937). I have never heard of him and can thus learn something before the train comes. Dossena was an Italian sculptor with the gift of living in each period of art history. He did not copy, he lived in it. He could work as an Etruscan or medieval or Victorian sculptor, and because he had not only a special handicraft but also a great knowledge of materials, it happened that in 1924 a dealer (a middleman!) entered the Museum of Fine Arts in Boston with a marble sarcophagus attributed to Mino da Fiesole (1429–1484), and sold it for 6 million lire (2.3 million euros). The sculptor himself received 25,000 lire (9,600 euros), for the guiding principle of trade is fraud (summed up in three words: *supply and demand*). After a delay, the sculptor found out that he had been swindled, and the story goes that, provoked by this financial disparity, he went to a judge in Rome (with photos of the work in progress) in order to get a settlement. This did not turn out well, he was regarded as a forger and had to justify himself in court. There he defended himself with a strong argument: his craftsmanship was not recognized as long as he worked under his own name, but when he imitated old art, no one saw the difference. He was no forger, he was merely recreating sculptures. He said: "I was born in our time, but with the soul, taste, and perception of other eras." The judge saw the soundness of this argument, he regarded it as a sort of crime passionnel and dropped the criminal proceedings against the artist.

The man in the station restaurant looks at me triumphantly, as though he himself had handed down the ruling in this case. He says: "This is really superior jurisprudence, we here in Northern Europe really couldn't even come close to it, could we?" I ask him what became of Dossena—was he honored as a great sculptor and did he live on as a prince? No, he died destitute in a poor-house hospital. In 1955, his son published a book with fifty-one photos of artwork produced by his father, with mention of the museums which show these works as authentic. The train comes into the station, I shake hands with the man, it is raining gently, I travel over the drizzly Veluwe to my destination. I live in Northern Europe.

DITHERING AND DALLYING

Today, a story about an event. The event is the receipt of a letter written by someone I lost touch with more than forty years ago, a vanished someone. In the sixties we worked in the same warehouse on the Oudezijds Achterburgwal. He made sculptures out of iron and wood, I also made sculptures out of iron and wood. He welded using electricity, I welded autogenously. My workshop was on the top floor at the front of the warehouse. I would hoist up the long gas cylinders with a heavy electric engine and was always afraid the thing would shoot out of the sling and explode like a bomb among the whores' clients down below. This never happened.

In 1971 I left for the Achterhoek. I had bought a VW Transporter in Friesland for two hundred guilders which I drove to my new house three hundred times, until the warehouse was empty. To the stupefaction of helpers and onlookers I took everything with me, even rusty nails and unusable wood chips. The vanished young man had recently seen the film by Joost Conijn on television and recognized me. In his letter he told me that he had at some time borrowed my professional belt sander, and that he had had a set of belts made for it which he still used.

I used the machine (a beautiful, heavy, reliable piece of equipment) for one year, then in 1972 the only belt tore and I didn't immediately know where I could have a new one made, I was not yet fully settled in. Whenever I needed the machine, I would resolve to do some research. Anyone who knows my character will not be surprised that for more than forty years now the belt sander has been waiting for me to order a new sanding belt.

That will happen, the letter struck a chord, I'm going to a sanding belt shop this afternoon, there must be an end to this dithering and dallying.

EIGHTEEN KILOMETERS

The artist Harm van der Wal asks if he can do a series of portraits of me. I think "why would he want to do that?" but I say "yes, all right." He comes eighteen kilometers on his bicycle because he does not own a car and although the public transportation is public it does not operate everywhere. So I receive him hospitably and offer him a whole-grain sandwich with cheese and a cup of black coffee. He asks if I will pose for him for two and a half hours in the attic of the house. This attic is twenty-seven meters long and fourteen meters wide, it is also completely empty, it is not an attic full of clutter. The clutter is in the house, the attic is empty. When my neighbor says that with me the world is upside down, I say, not without pride: you're right. The artist and I go upstairs, he has a thick roll of paper with him, a pointed stick from the woods, and a bottle of Indian ink. I'm carrying an improvised small table and a kitchen chair. I also have pen and paper with me, and a list of names of people who are expecting a letter from me about one thing and another. The artist unrolls the paper and does the portraits sitting on the floor. We are silent for two and a half hours. By then he has finished nine portraits and I five letters. The portraits are very lifelike, I have never before seen drawings made with a pointed piece of wood. I read him one of my letters out loud, three pages to a woman who is spreading rumors that I'm slow and sluggish. After that I take Harm van der Wal home in my car, eighteen kilometers. I have put the bicycle upright in the cargo area, supported by lashing straps that are meant for this. The artist compliments me on making such good sailor's knots.

THE HEART OF THE STORY

KRO radio asked if I would be willing to write a very short Christmas story. I have written a Christmas story on request before, but still, in this case I felt especially honored. After all, the Catholics invented Christmas, and in particular the little crèche, with its Catholic ox and ass. And by the way, there are more reasons for being grateful to the Catholics. What would Gerard Reve, Sam Rodia, and John Fante have been without this great carnival faith.

Out of gratitude I situated the story in Amsterdam West, the part of town where the most Catholics live. Off the top of my head, I can already think of two I know there, Dennis Bergkamp and Kees Fens. I myself have always been afraid of this neighborhood because of its suffocating dullness. I never went into Amsterdam North or East, but I did go into Amsterdam West. In Witte de Withstraat I was tutored in math by a man who received me in a dreary little side room where there was barely space for a foldaway bed. After I had read "Spider" out loud on a second Christmas Day, I realized that my fear of Amsterdam West lies at the heart of the story and that no listener had any idea of that. Kees Fens would have understood it, but Dennis Bergkamp probably doesn't listen to Radio 4. He also doesn't read newspapers or books, I've heard that he even left his own biography unread.

SPIDER (A CHRISTMAS TALE)

We sometimes wonder how and when it began. Then we think of our oldest sister, she turned twenty that year, 1958. At the beginning of December she told our parents she no longer wanted to celebrate Christmas. It came as a shock to an upstanding Catholic household in Amsterdam West, six children, two girls, four boys, father an administrator at the Markthallen, mother a housewife, nothing to find fault with. Modest participants in the Silent Walk. Our oldest sister, Rosalie, had discovered that the Christmas celebration had nothing to do with faith, it was established on the date of a pagan festival, it had degenerated into eating and drinking. A couple of weeks later she went one step further, she wanted to leave home, she wanted to go south, where none of us had ever been. She would make a fresh start, she would leave not only her family and her faith, she would also leave our country and our climate—though the sixties hadn't even begun yet. There was great confusion among both the parents and the children, the order had been upset for the first time. They tried to talk to Rosalie, they warned, threatened, wept and implored, but she remained unexpectedly obstinate. At last she left, and our father comforted himself with the thought that if she had a change of heart near Maastricht, she could always still borrow ten guilders from someone, then she would be back home before supper.

But that didn't happen, Rosalie was seized with wanderlust. It was unthinkable that she could remain living in Amsterdam West— without anyone noticing, she had been standing on the springboard all these years, and in December 1958 she sprang. She passed Maastricht without faltering, left the Forest of Ardennes and Alsace behind and in January ended up in Southern France, where she met a sculptor who made iron sculptures. She stayed there living with him for ten years and then crossed the Mediterranean. Since then she has lived in Africa. All the rest of us have moved, too, only my younger sister still lives in Amsterdam West. No one still joins the Silent Walk, I believe that only my brother is of the opinion that "there must be something," but what exactly he means by that, I don't know. In the sixties I once went to visit Rosalie and her sculptor. In the yard next to the studio stood gigantic iron sculptures. A spider seven meters high made the deepest impression. I won't say that I understood everything when I saw the creature, but what was quite clear to me was that one couldn't go on living in Amsterdam West.

NIGHT TRAIN

When Meindert Vermeer awakes at six o'clock in the morning (always without an alarm clock) he looks at a photo of a squirrel drinking from a dripping faucet in the kitchen. His father took the photo in his forest home in Doorn. He lived there alone, which he did not like, he was looking for a wife. He didn't know how to accomplish this, he was an eccentric for whom the most ordinary things were unattainable. The shy squirrel, however, did not run away when he walked into the kitchen. The little creature recognized the animal within the man and, unperturbed, even allowed itself to be photographed. Meindert owes his existence to two words—*night train*. His father had decided to look for his wife in a night train. For this he traveled in a shabby tour bus to Marseille, where he took the night train to Brussels. He later told his son what the rationale for this plan was. If he had taken the night train from Utrecht to the South of France, fate would not have been set in motion. The woman would have to be sitting in a train that was traveling in the direction of the Netherlands, she had to be on her way to our country. In order to trick fate, he therefore rode in an anonymous bus to the departure point of the night train. Fate was merciful to him, in the train he did indeed sit next to a woman he liked, but she said nothing to him, she couldn't be bothered, he even thought she wasn't aware of his presence. But because it was a night train, she fell asleep with her head on his shoulder. They were married in Brussels—Meindert was born in the forest house in Doorn.

GEESE

For the past few days there have been two geese in the fields around our house. I am not yet used to them. Sometimes their noise is so far away that I don't know if I am really hearing it, perhaps they have never actually been here. I doubt myself, yet the elephant that walked through the garden here yesterday was so large, I could not have invented him?

The fact is, in high school I did acquire a fear of making things up. I had a realistic teacher of Dutch literature who wanted an essay to be based on absolute reality. As soon as he guessed that you had made something up, he would give you an F. Yet I liked him, he believed that film was not an art because you could not decide what you as spectator were looking at, the filmmaker was the boss. In theater, on the other hand, you could decide which part of the stage you would look at and which actor you would pay special attention to. A strange and eccentric theory that could easily be refuted, but not by me, for he found me rude and irritating, he never listened to my interruptions. Because of his madness I consider him a good teacher, one who has remained in my memory. If he had confined himself to the prescribed curriculum, he would have disappeared into the mists of time. That will also happen, but only after my death, for I sometimes think about him. And as long as I do that, he is still alive.

LITTLE DOG

Kees is driving on the A1 when his phone rings. This is a special moment, because it is the first time in his life. He bought the cell phone the day before. The salesperson told him not to telephone when his hands were on the steering wheel. Kees drives over into the Tolnegen parking area and sees that his son Jan has called him. That does not surprise him, Jan is the only one who knows the number. Jan is sixty-three years old, his father is eighty-three. Jan addresses his father with the first words spoken into the telephone by the inventor Alexander Graham Bell in 1876 to his assistant Thomas Watson: "Mr. Watson, come here."

As Kees remains sitting for a while longer after this conversation, glowing, there is a tap at his window. It is a young woman who asks if she can hitch a ride, she needs to go to Amsterdam. On the way, he asks her if, after the incidents in Cologne and Sweden, she is not afraid of men. She says: "No, because I always have my little dog with me." Only then does Kees see the head of the very small, full-grown dog that she is carrying under her jacket. The woman was born in our country of Spanish parents, from her mouth speak the Phoenicians, the Romans, the Moors, the Greeks, and the Egyptian pharaohs. He is dizzied by her mythological stories, Cologne and Sweden shatter under her force, her little dog appears to be thousands of years old. He drops her off by the Rijksmuseum and drives himself with throbbing temples to the Hobbemakade, where he lives, and calms down. In the evening, he listens to *Verklärte Nacht* by Arnold Schoenberg.

IN THE ELM TREES

After the storm I cycle through the woods to see if the Vrauw-deunt family is still in the land of the living. I'm friends with this couple, Janus and Emilie Vrauwdeunt. Their humble little house lies deep in the woods, reachable only by those who know the way. So many trees have blown down that after a hundred meters I can no longer get through with my bicycle. I leave it behind and go scrambling on. The house was not struck, but it was a close call, Janus and Emilie are already sawing with a large two-person saw dating from World War II. They were in fact born before the war, Janus in 1935, Emilie in 1936. They are sober people, they are old but do not yet make use of the neighborhood care system. I would like to congratulate them, but I don't do that, it is not for nothing that they have lived more than half a century in great solitude. They nod to me and continue sawing. Later, when weariness has won out, they invite me into the kitchen after all, to have a cup of coffee. What kind of tree are you sawing, I ask. An elm, says Emilie, but we call it an olm. An owl appears in my brain: "The owl sat in the elm trees ..." My memory refuses to cooperate any further, Emilie helps me: "... as the night was falling, and back of yonder hills came soft the cuckoo calling." After the coffee they continue sawing, but I am left with the sudden mystery of yonder hills.

EXPERIMENT

The man I want to say something about almost never went outside when he was young, nor did his brothers and sisters. They lived in a large apartment on the top floor of a skyscraper, the world lay at their feet. Their parents were educated people, they taught their children themselves. The old money was in a safe account. The bookcases were full, there were radios and gramophone records. There was no television (then in its infancy). The man I'm talking about I met in the hospital on Prinsengracht, where he and I lay in a ward for people who had had appendectomies. He was twenty years old and had just moved out of his parents' house. He was studying law. I listened with astonishment to his stories and wanted to know if his parents were of sound mind, but I did not dare ask him that, since I had known him for only two days. The day before we were to be released, he said one more sentence about it: "It was an experiment of my father's." After that, I saw him one more time, forty years later, during the intermission of a Russian opera. He had become a lawyer, successful, with a large clientele. His wife was a doctor, his children were students. The same was true of his brothers and sisters, accomplished, respectable lives. He looked at me mockingly. "You wouldn't give a cent for it back then, in the hospital. You're a person with fixed and predictable patterns, I already noticed that back then." While I thought about this, the bell rang, we had to return for the last part of the Russian opera. I never saw him again.

IDEALISM

The girl from the novel is standing by the ice cream maker in the marketplace, exactly as I was told. I can't believe it, it's really her, in the flesh. The novel exists too, I had it in my hand, I had read it unsuspectingly during a vacation in Italy, thirty years ago. That I forgot the book when I left, abandoned it in the hotel room, I consider to be a painful detail. When I discovered this and called the hotel a day later, it had disappeared. I don't think it's a very good book, but the girl is irresistible. She has chosen not to waste her life in paltry pleasures and superficial display, she really wants to commit herself to the wretched of the earth. And that's how it happens, she goes to South America and ends up working for a Catholic priest who runs a home in which he takes under his wing abandoned and runaway children. But before that, she must end the relationship with her fiancé. He is charming, caustic, intelligent, and even an aristocrat. The condition of the world does not interest him. Life is short, there is only time for pleasure. Naturally this is the main part of the book, her struggle to make this vital choice. The girl who has serious doubts, the fiancé who does not understand and in the end waves goodbye to her at Schiphol Airport with a new girlfriend on his arm.

Years later I hear from someone who is a specialist in the test kitchen of literature—the personal dramas, the sad details, the cheerful notes, the backbiting and treachery—that the main character of what I will simply call my Italian novel lives near me, in the area, thirty years older but still alive and kicking and undefeated.

I see her standing there, she's the wife of the ice cream maker, it doesn't matter who she's with, priest, count, or vendor. I don't dare speak to her, I would run the risk of making a lousy joke about idealism. I remain at a distance looking at her.

POEM

In the silent woods behind my house I am always afraid because there are no people there and I often imagine, also, that behind my back I hear, coming from the low undergrowth, music by Arvo Pärt. Yesterday I saw a person walking there whom I knew, fortunately, it was Wouter Vos, his wife was walking behind him, she was having trouble with the muddy footpath. I heard her say: "It's all right, I'm coming, don't worry."

Wouter said to me: "A wife like this, who doesn't object to the mud on the path, is a supremely good companion, a companion who isn't afraid of life."

They live a few kilometers to the east in a run-down tower that suffered quite a lot of damage during the last storm. Wouter is a retired customs officer, his wife studied literature in Tokyo, where she did her PhD on Kawabata. From her I heard the delicate story about Yasunari Kawabata, who in 1968 was surprised to receive the Nobel Prize in Literature. When all the visitors had gone he wrote a poem:

> Invisible he
> who will walk with ringing bells
> through the autumn fields.

Ever since then, I have known this poem by heart, not long ago I also used it as a form of currency. I was staying in a hotel in the center of Leuven, in Maria Theresiastraat, across from a large, old-fashioned prison with stout bars on the windows. Early in the morning I was warned that a traffic policeman was standing next to my car—parked in the wrong place. He was a young agent with a large motorbike whose praises I would happily have sung. I explained to him which parking signs had confused me. He granted me forgiveness and I recited for him then and there Kawabata's poem.

SENTENCE

The advantage of a car is that you can travel undisturbed, on your own. The disadvantage of a car is that you don't meet any strangers and are always stuck with yourself, which in the long run is not enough. This week I was once again sitting on a train, and I heard a man say to a woman, "You have to come to terms with death, that's what you have to do." I found it a powerful, stand-alone sentence, which on closer examination would have no meaning in daily life. I did not have to take the train more often for that, but I was happy I had heard it.

I thought that perhaps I could also have heard this sentence six hundred years ago on a pilgrimage through Northern Spain or in a little boat on the Ganges. But a medievalist friend disenchanted me, there were no such sentences in the Middle Ages, people had something else on their minds.

But another friend, a spiritual man who had been a Roman Catholic in his youth and later turned to Hinduism, thought it was indeed possible that such a sentence was uttered in India. After his conversion he had lived for years in that country, and right near the Ganges, in which he often bathed. On his next visit, perhaps in the autumn of this year, he would ask the river if it had ever heard anyone murmur this sentence.

THE QUESTION

When I am doing my grocery shopping at four in the afternoon in the supermarket by the harbor basin I meet the Chinese man there. I have known him for nine years, I've never met him anywhere else but in this supermarket and never at any other time of the day than four o'clock. He has a twin brother who owns a large import-export firm in Singapore. He is so rich that he has his own airplane. The brothers look very much alike, both embarked on the same projects with the same results. When they were sixteen years old, they wanted to write a magnificent poem, but that didn't work out, they had no poet's blood in them. Then they tried hiking, they bought the official hiking costume and prepared to follow the course of the Yellow River. After two weeks, they met a hermit who predicted that this walking trip would fail because they were not wearing the right outfits. They gave up on their journey and decided to attempt one more project. They planted a large garden. In the beginning it went well, but they were not able to sustain it, they weren't strong enough to plow. They were twenty-five years old and decided to go their separate ways. One went off to Singapore, where he became so rich that by the time he was forty he owned his own airplane. The other went to the Netherlands, where he became, in his own words, "expert at daily living." They were now seventy-five years old and still in regular touch with each other. I asked the Dutch Chinese man which life was now a success. He answered that they did not ask each other such questions, because if you don't pose the question you also don't have to give an answer.

PUSSYFOOT

The man near the ship did not give the least sign of recognition. I hesitated, I did not know if I could still trust myself. They are not words to me, but I'll utter them anyway: I was experiencing an existential confusion. I was with this man in Amsterdam, once, picking up a harpsichord in my delivery van. He lived on the ship in a small port in the Twentekanaal. Before we left Amsterdam, he asked me to stop somewhere near the Montelbaanstoren, where he had one more thing to do. He went onto a large, gray, uninhabited ship, I followed him and saw to my dismay enormous terrariums containing large snakes to which he was feeding live mice. Death on the water. Later I heard him play the harpsichord again, civilized music that I could not dissociate from the snakes and the mice. Now I'm skipping over thirty years, unfortunately I have that option, time is like wax in my hands. I'm in the harbor one evening, I see the ship, I see a light in the cabin, I'm unsuspecting as always and knock. He opens, is friendly, but does not recognize me. To be honest, I recognize him only because I know the ship. I present the problem to him, we agree to talk to each other without any intention of recognizing each other. We do that, we drink wine and don't force anything, we let fate, so-called, do the work. Mankind should not interfere with everything. It takes quite some time for the Montelbaanstoren, the snakes, and the harpsichord to open the way. And then not even with an Ah or an Oh, there is no sudden breakthrough, we are embarrassed by the pussyfooting march of time.

BEES

I have no bedside table, the books lie next to the bed in piles on the floor, a paper city seen from above. Among them is *Mijn naam is Legioen* (My name is Legion), poems by Menno Wigman. In the night they sometimes leap out of their collection into my head. For example, the poem "M," in which Rodolfus Glaber writes that in June of the year one thousand a man, tired from working on the land, fell forward and dreamed that a great swarm of bees squeezed through the openings in his body. Because of this poem the night can no longer be avoided, sleep becomes unattainable, and I have to think about bees. In the newspaper, I regularly read that bees are sick and that because they will disappear, humans will also disappear from the earth.

Although I live in the country, I'm no country person, I'm a city person, I know the sound the tram made in the 1950s entering the bend at Roelof Hartplein. And here in the silence of the Achterhoek I watch like a stranger the bees that fly from flower to flower. From the man who prunes my trees—he's also a beekeeper, he owns colonies of bees—I hear that bees gather their honey mainly from flowering trees, he gives me a little pot of Dutch linden honey. And then once again a coincidence: the girl from Amsterdam. I have seen her two or three times. She comes for a visit and gives me a little pot of Herengracht honey, extracted that same morning by her friend. I turn into a question mark, she explains it, he keeps bees on the roof terrace of his house on the Herengracht. Later, when she is back in North Holland, I try to think what kinds of trees grow along the Herengracht. Maybe you can tell by the taste.

HUMAN AND ANIMAL

I'm sitting in the Kennemer Dunes at a wooden table. There are no people, only seagulls, two of them. They are large, they have yellow beaks, their eyes, cold and motionless, go back to the beginning of humankind's mythology, they came out of the Pacific Ocean to the Kennemer Dunes just yesterday. This is the situation, they walk along the path of shells, ten meters away.

On the plastic plate lie two brown sandwiches of roast beef and fried egg, the sun is shining, but it is cold, it is April, the cruel month that does not betray its promise. I stand up in order to go get some salt from the caravan, I hear the inaudible behind my back, I turn around, I sprint, each seagull has a sandwich with egg and roast beef in its beak, they float on their wings, two, three meters high. I understand the history of humans and animals, I resign myself to it.

WOOD

For fifty years I've been collecting wood for the stove, which stands like a telephone booth in the room, I look back with amazement. Now for the first time I have bought some wood. There are exotic pieces among them that are invincible, even the heaviest ax has difficulty with them. The seller who came to bring the wood was born in Clermont-Ferrand. He had a wood business there too. I told him I had once had car trouble in the vicinity of Clermont. While I was taken by taxi to the Volkswagen garage in the industrial area, I chatted with the driver, who was driving very fast. I sat next to him and looked tensely out at the traffic. He was driving twenty centimeters from the car ahead of him and had the habit of turning his face toward me when he said something. Twice he had to brake with all his might, predictably, for the driver in front of him was a little old woman, and little old women were, according to him, the source of all traffic problems. He asked me if he should give her a "tap," but I strongly advised against it. I had to stay in Clermont a few more days and so I also sometimes took the public bus. On it, I once sat next to an attractive, vulgar young woman who was on the phone with her lover. She did not lower her voice and regularly said, "Je t'embrasse partout." ("I kiss you all over.") Later, just to be sure, I looked up *embrasser*: kiss, cuddle, hug, caress, embrace, entwine. I considered telling her that the word "partout" in this connection was inappropriate on public transport, but my knowledge of their language and customs was too crude for that sort of interference.

The man who had brought the wood asked if I was a democrat at heart. I answered that I have voted all my life, even when I found it a shameful spectacle. I asked if he had ever heard of Ezra Pound. He certainly had, after all he had attended French schools. You learn more there than in Dutch schools. So he knew that Ezra Pound is considered the greatest poet of the twentieth century.

From 1941 to 1945, several times a week, that man bellowed fascist messages out into the world through the Italian radio microphone, scabby black birds with strong beaks. What should you say about that? I can't break free from the respectable democratic upbringing I had at home and at school. I can laugh about Ezra Pound, his deranged *furor*, but if I had to choose, I'd rather opt for democracy anyway.

The wood man agreed. He would come back when I needed wood again.

FREE

It began with trees, it ends with stones. Free. Forty years ago I saw a heap of conifers with their root balls on the side of a sandy road in the woods. On a piece of pale cardboard in barely legible letters: Free. I was excited and felt shamefully greedy. I cycled back home fast, fifteen kilometers, hooked the trailer onto the back of the car and drove anxiously back, fifteen kilometers. Relief, the coast was clear, no pirates.

Today the five pines with their dead-straight trunks stick up well above the house. I estimate them to be twelve meters high. When I look at the trunks every morning, on my way to the chicken coop, I always think of the sailing ships in which the Spanish, the English, and the Dutch fought one another. How thick they are I don't know, I've never measured them. I will do that now, for once in my life I want to make an exact, verifiable statement, I go look for a tape measure. [...] Done, circumference 135 centimeters, there is sap on the tape measure and on my fingers, I go clean my hands with a brush, I must keep my computer free of sap. Sap is a dangerous enemy of the keyboard.

The stones stood piled up by the side of a paved road, a couple of weeks ago, also with the statement that one could take them for free. There are many of them, I drove back four or five times. They stand like a solid block in a corner of our grounds, I do not see them every day, I could forget them. I could also make an Assyrian lion gate out of them or a romantic English-style winding path. It doesn't matter, I am a slave to the word "free." I'm aware of it, but I can't do anything about it.

LINTEL

The man is working in an old barn two stories high. He is alone, the barn stands in a solitary mountainous area of Southern France. He is busy preparing a buttress against a lofty, bulging inner wall. He is a quiet man, he does not talk much, he has turned his back on the frenzy of the world. He reads no newspapers, he has no television, he has no children, his wife has left him after five years of marriage and gone off to live in a big city to make up for the time she had wasted. In the evenings he sometimes listens to the music of Morton Feldman, but usually even that is too much for him and he sits motionless in the silent house.

While he is busy with the foundation of the abutment he hears little nibbling sounds, he drops the trowel in the mortar and straightens up—he is hearing the building breathe. It is ten meters to the outer door, ten meters between life and death. As the building collapses he is saved by the tough, old, arched lintel of the door. No one can see him standing there while things quiet down again, a medieval saint in the frame of a painting.

BANANA

When our country was still a bit untidier and so a bit more livable, at the back side of society stood bins of discarded food. People with pigs could take them away. I had two addresses: the kitchen of the police academy where I was a teacher and the Albert Heijn supermarket in the village where I live. At the school a great deal was eaten and so a great deal thrown away. Cooked and baked foods, soups and sauces, the pigs found it delectable. This food source was the first to be prohibited by the authorities, swine fever had been detected, the soups and sauces were blamed. For a while, the garbage bin of the Albert Heijn remained out of harm's way. In it there were vegetables and fruit, carefully wrapped, from all over the world, a sum of cheap labor, the price of kerosene and honest entrepreneurship. So I know how a pig eats an apple, a pear, or an oyster mushroom, he sticks his snout into the trough and slobbers up the whole business like a dredger. Two exceptions, the banana and the acorn. I live at the edge of an oak forest, I used to gather acorns for the pigs.

A pig holds an acorn very precisely in the front of his mouth, the way I imagine a lady in a literary salon eats a bonbon while she listens to a young poet. But the banana is his crowning achievement. He pushes it and moves his snout back and forth, very delicately, like an instrument maker, until the fruit bursts open over its entire length, and then he feasts with pleasure on the sweet, pale thing. If I ever, God forbid, end up in an old people's home, that will be my glory, that I'm the only one of the mumblers who knows how a pig eats a banana.

Notes

GRANDSON

Jan Wolkers: Dutch writer, sculptor, and painter (1925–2007) who for two years appeared in a gardening program in which he explored his own backyard on the island of Texel and talked, in a whimsical but informative way, about the plants and animals that thrived there.

YEARS

Vertigo: a cafe named after the Hitchcock film located on the edge of Amsterdam's Vondelpark in the vaulted basement of the nineteenth-century villa housing the Dutch Film Museum.

FOX

Wytze Hellinga: Dutch bibliographer and linguist (1908–1985), known particularly for his editions of the Middle Dutch epic Reynaert the Fox.

OX

Geert Wilders: a right-wing Dutch politician.

SHOE

Zkv: stands for zeer kort verhaal, or "very short story." Snijders invented this term for the short form in which he customarily writes. It has by now gained currency among other writers of the form in Dutch.

Wytze Hellinga: see "Fox."

HURT TO THE BONE

Wildschut: a spacious, well-known, centrally located Art Deco bar/cafe popular with both Amsterdam locals and tourists.

RESENTMENT

Jan Kalff: prominent Dutch banker.

SUMMER

Peter R. de Vries: Dutch investigative journalist, crime reporter, and host of a popular true-crime television program. In 2005, he started his own political party, but he disbanded it soon after when he found he did not have enough popular support.

BAALBEK

An archaeological site in Lebanon, known in Roman times as Heliopolis, or City of the Sun.

NOTE

Karel van het Reve: a Dutch writer, translator, and literary historian (1921–1999), considered one of the finest Dutch essayists.

Benya Krik: a fictional Russian Jewish gangster who figures prominently in Isaac Babel's collection of short stories *The Odessa Tales*.

BALDUR

CV: the title of a book by Carel Helder (CH).

LUCK

Kees Otten: an internationally known recorder player, with many concerts, LPs, and CDs to his credit. He died in 2008.

Vondelpark: a large park in the west of Amsterdam.

The Overtoom: a neighborhood in the west of Amsterdam

ULK

Achterhoeks: a dialect of Dutch Low Saxon which is spoken in the north-eastern Netherlands.

Polecat: a mainly nocturnal European carnivorous mammal of the weasel family.

ROZENSTRAAT

The Afsluitdijk: a major causeway separating the North Sea from the IJs-selmeer, in the north of Holland, thirty-two kilometers long and nine meters wide.

WOOL CAP

One of the first pieces of writing in the Dutch language (about 1050–1075) is a fragment—a scribble in the margin of a Latin manuscript, a copyist apparently trying out his pen—that reads: "All the birds have begun their nests, except you and me. What are we waiting for?"

The two translations of the Japanese poem are almost the same. The differences are these:

Snijders: *herfst*: autumn

Flip: *herfsttij*: literally, "waning," maybe "the waning of the season"

Snijders: *ik ga nergens naartoe*: I go nowhere

Flip: *ik ga nergens heen*: I go nowhere

They mean the same thing but *naartoe* is neater (and more formal) than *heen*

Snijders: *niemand komt mij bezoeken*: no one comes to visit me

Flip: *niemand komt langs*: no one comes by.

The bat referred to at the end of the story appears in another story by Snijders called "Bat."

CARBIDE

In the Netherlands, it is traditional to create carbide explosions on New Year's Eve, putting calcium carbide and water inside a closed milk can and ignitng the gasses thus created. This may originally have been a pagan ritual to drive away bad spirits.

SEVENTEENTH CENTURY

Frits Grönloh: real name of "Nescio" (1882–1961), one of Snijders's favorite Dutch writers.

Hoogaars: a seventeenth-century Dutch fishing boat with a rectangular mainsail; it originated in the Zeeland province of the Netherlands.

GENERATIVE GRAMMER

"*Suzanne*": a poem by Willem Frederik Hermans (1921–1995), who is considered one of the three most important postwar authors in the Netherlands, along with Harry Mulisch and Gerard Reve. His works include novels, short stories, plays, poetry, essays, photographs, and writings on philosophy and science.

St. Joost ten Noode: one of the nineteen municipalities located in the Brussels-Capital Region of Belgium.

EGGS

Waddenzee: Dutch, "mud flats sea"—a constantly changing landscape situated in an intertidal zone in the southeastern part of the North Sea and including mud flats, tidal creeks, and islands.

He had taken eggs for his money: a Dutch expression ("Eieren kiezen voor je geld") that means to accept a different form of currency, or to be content with something of lesser value, but safer; or to play it safe. Also: to allow oneself to be imposed upon. The expression once existed in English, also—common in the sixteenth century—meaning to accept an offer one would rather refuse, as when, for instance, a shopkeeper felt obliged to accept eggs as well as cash for small purchases. (See Shakespeare, *Winter's Tale*: "Mine honest friend, Will you take eggs for money?")

HELPLESS BECAUSE OF RESPECT

Jaffe Vink: Dutch philosopher and writer who for some years edited the "letter and spirit" section of the daily newspaper *Trouw* (Fidelity), which was started during WWII by the Dutch Protestant resistance movement.

Max Frisch: Swiss playwright and novelist (1911–1991), some of whose major themes are personal identity and moral and ethical questions.

The closing couplet is from "Borms," a 1947 poem by Willem Elsschot, pen name of Alfons de Ridder (1882–1960), a Flemish writer and poet whose classic novel *Cheese* has recently been translated into English by Paul Vincent; the poem is about August Borms, a Flemish nationalist leader executed for collaborating with the German occupying forces during WWII.

LITTLE BOX

Dragonfly man: in another story, "Common Redstart," Snijders tells of a stranger who comes past the house to enter the woods and photograph dragonflies in a pool of water. This man over time becomes something of a friend.

FORTY CENTIMETERS

Blokker's: large Dutch chain store carrying household goods, pet supplies, etc.

Gerrit Krol: innovative, inventive, and prolific Dutch author (1934–2013) of novels, novellas, short stories, essays, columns on science, philosophy, and literature; winner, in 1986, of the Constantijn Huygens Prize for his complete works and, in 2001, of the P. C. Hooft Award for Literature, the Netherlands' most important literary award.

TOWN LINE

Willem Elsschot: pen name of Alfons de Ridder, Flemish novelist, short-story writer, and poet. *Villa des Roses* was written in 1913 and brought Elsschot to public attention (see also the note for "Helpless Because of Respect").

Anthonis de Roovere: Flemish poet (1430–1482) and member of the *rederijkerskamer* (rhetoric and elocution society) of Bruges. He was best known for his ballads, rondels, and refrains.

Vanitas poem: poem on the theme of the futility and transience of earthly life

Nicolaas Matsier: pen name of Tjit Reinsma, a Dutch novelist awarded the Ferdinand Bordewijk Prize in 1995 for his novel *Gesloten huis* (Locked House), and a friend of Snijders's.

CHRISTMAS 13

Jules Renard: French writer (1864–1910). Most famous works: *Poil de Carotte* (1894) and *Les Histoires Naturelles* (1896). These translations from the journal of Jules Renard benefit from the renderings into English by Louise Bogan and Elizabeth Roget.

Martinus Nijhoff: important twentiethth-century Dutch poet and essayist (1894–1953), much admired by Snijders for his formal virtuosity, intense spirituality, and original imagery.

A WOMAN

Till Eulenspiegel: a trickster figure originating in Middle Low German folklore. In the stories, he is presented as a traveler who plays practical jokes on his contemporaries, exposing vices at every turn: greed and folly, hypocrisy and foolishness. In a large number of the tales his wit is based on his literal interpretation of figurative language.

OH MY BRIDE

VPRO: a broadcasting corporation in the Netherlands that typically produces and broadcasts high-level, somewhat avant-garde, programming and whose target audience could be considered to be mainly intellectuals and creative people.

Temee: the English equivalent of this word does not appear in Smith's original; presumably *temee* was added to the Dutch translation to maintain the rhyme scheme. In the original, the old man is seventy-three; in the translation he is eighty.

Van Dale: the classic, or standard, Dutch-English dictionary, compiled by J. H. van Dale and based on a previous dictionary by I. M. Calisch and N. S. Calisch. It was first published in 1874 and is regularly updated.

The Jordaan: a neighborhood of Amsterdam, once working-class.

DITHERING AND DALLYING

Oudezijds Achterburgwal: a street and canal in De Wallen, the red-light district in the center of Amsterdam.

Autogenously: done either without solder or with a filler of the same metal as the pieces being welded.

The Achterhoek: a large area within the Dutch province of Gelderland.

The film by Joost Conijn: Joost Conijn (b. 1971) is an artist, filmmaker and writer. He is known for his projects with self-made machines, examining the boundaries between human beings and technology. He made a fifty-minute film called "Een handige dromer" (A handy dreamer) about Snijders, visiting him at his home in the Achterhoek.

EIGHTEEN KILOMETERS

Harm van der Wal: an internationally exhibited mixed-media artist (b. 1950) exploring the interaction of nature and culture.

THE HEART OF THE STORY

Gerard Reve: Dutch writer (1923–2006) considered (along with Willem Frederik Hermans and Harry Mulisch) one of the "Great Three" of postwar Dutch literature. He was openly gay and a devout Catholic.

Sam Rodia: also known as Simon Rodia (born 1879 in Italy, died 1965 in Martinez, California), he was a construction worker and mason who built the Watts Towers in Los Angeles, designated a National Historic Landmark in 1990.

John Fante: American novelist, short-story writer, and screenwriter (1909–1983) best known for his grimly realistic novel *Ask the Dust* about a struggling writer in Depression-era Los Angeles. Along with poverty, family life, sports, the writing life, and the Italian-American identity, Catholicism was a recurring theme in his work.

Kees Fens: prizewinning Dutch writer, essayist, and literary critic (1929–2008), a devout Catholic.

Dennis Bergkamp: famous Dutch professional soccer coach and former player (b. 1969) who was a member of the national soccer team.

Radio 4: a classical-music station on which Snijders reads a story every Sunday morning.

Silent Walk: called the Stille Omgang in Dutch, this is an informal Catholic ritual repeated in Amsterdam every March to commemorate a Eucharistic miracle of 1345. Thousands of people from all over the Netherlands take part in it following evening Mass in one of Amsterdam's churches.

LITTLE DOG

Incidents in Cologne and Sweden: on New Year's Eve 2015–2016, in Cologne, hundreds of women were molested in group attacks by several dozen men described as North African and Arab; in Sweden, at the We Are Stockholm music festival, girls were surrounded by groups of young men, primarily refugees from Afghanistan, and sexually harassed.

Hobbemakade: a quayside residential area in the Oud Zuid district of Amsterdam named after the seventeenth-century Dutch painter Meindert Hobbema.

IN THE ELM TREES

Neighborhood care system: this is known as *Buurtzorg* in Dutch. It is a innovative district nursing and home care organization in the Netherlands started in 2006 and employing nurses organized in teams of up to twelve responsible for forty to sixty people within a particular area.

Elm . . . olm: there are two words in Dutch for "elm"—the first word Emilie uses is *iep* and second is *olm*. In the song, the word used (in the plural) is *olmen*.

The owl sat in the elm trees: "De uil zat in de olmen," a traditional Dutch folk song in the form of a canon.

PUSSYFOOT

The Twentekanaal: a sixty-five-kilometer-long canal in the eastern central Netherlands that runs through the provinces of Gelderland and Overijssel. Snijders's hometown has a harbor next to the Twentekanaal.

The Montelbaanstoren: a tower on the bank of Amsterdam's Oude Schans canal, the oldest part of which was built in 1516 as part of a defensive wall for protecting the eastern side of the harbor.

An Ah or an Oh: a reference to "Ah, the World! Oh, the World!" in *Moby-Dick*, and a phrase often quoted by Snijders, according to his Dutch publisher.

BEES

Roelof Hartplein: a square in Amsterdam where several streets come together. The first tram crossed the square in 1904.

Achterhoek: the mainly rural region where Snijders lives, in the easternmost part of the province of Gelderland and on the border with Germany. Its name translates literally as "back corner." It is an area of farmland and untouched nature—forests and sand flats.

Herengracht: a street that runs along the Herengracht canal, the most important in Amsterdam.

HUMAN AND ANIMAL

The Kennemer Dunes: an extensive, scenic, and peaceful hilly dune park on the Atlantic about half an hour from Amsterdam with many cycling and walking paths as well as a lake and beaches.

FREE

Pirates: there is an expression in Dutch, "er zijn kapers op de kust" (literally, "there are pirates on the coast") which means "we have competition." The expression dates back to the time of the Spanish seafaring marauders